JUDICIUM

DEVILS PLAYGROUND

NATALIE BENNETT

COPYRIGHT

BLURB

Tick tock...it's time for judgment.

The blood we spilled came after the riddles.

Betrayal followed by those we trusted.

There are so many things we could have done differently, saving ourselves from future heartache.

Now, it's too late to recast the die.

By everything tainted and maleficent, we're forever bonded.

Every tragedy has an origin.

This is where ours begins.

Contents

COPYRIGHT

BLURB

DEVIL'S PLAYGROUND

AUTHOR NOTE

PLAYLIST

CHAPTER ONE

CHAPTER TWO

CHAPTER THREE

CHAPTER FOUR

CHAPTER FIVE

CHAPTER SIX

CHAPTER SEVEN

CHAPTER EIGHT

CHAPTER NINE

CHAPTER TEN

EPILOGUE

CARMINE

More books from Natalie Bennett

Books from Mae Royal

THE SECT

NEFARIOUS

SOCIALS

DEVIL'S PLAYGROUND

PERICULUM

MALEFICIUM

JUDICIUM

DAEMONIUM-2023

OBSCURUM-2023

Coming Soon!

TORMENTUM: DEVIL'S PLAYGROUND:
U

AUTHOR NOTE

Hi!

Judicium is solely meant to fill in some of the backstory that precedes Periculum. It is purposely vague and more plot-driven than steamy. (I promise the final books will have plenty.) If you're reading this and new to the series, you're going to have a lot more questions than answers and probably be really confused. I highly recommend beginning with Periculum.

If you're a day one viewer of the Devil's Playground, you'll still have some questions, but you'll also get a few answers. There are plenty of easter eggs layered in here too for both this series and the spin-off. If you find you want to skip this one and go straight to Daemonium, that's fine too! You will not be left confused. Everything comes together by the end of Obscurum.

If you need a TW click here.

Happy reading!

PLAYLIST

CHAPTER ONE

This definitely wasn't how I saw my night going. If my parents found out where I was, I'd be helping them decide on my tombstone inscription and choosing a casket come morning.

With the way things were at home right now, maybe that wouldn't be such a bad thing. I didn't want to die but a vacation a few feet underground wasn't sounding too terrible.

I weaved around a couple that was practically dry humping in the middle of the makeshift dance floor, searching the mass of gyrating bodies for my sister. The sheer amount of people here made it hard to search for one specific person.

It would've been helpful if she told me what she had on. At the very least she could've relayed where I should go for us to meet up.

A guy dressed as a creepy pig bumped into me from behind, nearly knocking me down. The liquid in the cup I was holding sloshed over the side and onto my hand.

I steadied myself and glared at the back of his latex head as he shuffled by without offering an apology. He reeked of alcohol and something else. Why the hell was he even wearing a costume? Did he somehow confuse June with October?

Ugh. I hated everything about this situation. I hadn't seen or heard from my sister in nearly three weeks. The last time I saw her was when our mother quite literally threw her out of the house. She dragged her across the floor and through the front door.

It was one of the only times I'd seen her get physical with my siblings.

Fast forward to thirty minutes or so ago when I'd just stepped forward to order my large popcorn from the concession stand and she sent a random text asking me to meet her here.

Of course, I came. I don't know why she did though. Lamia had always loved to party but given her current predicament this wasn't anywhere she should be. Even I had declined tonight's invite. I knew there would be a larger crowd than usual given it was early summer.

Some of these people were fresh out of high school. Others were university students like Lamia. A few had graduated from both a long time ago and still made an appearance. I personally found that to be a little disturbing when it came to the guys looking to pick up girls.

I continued making my way around the room, every so often recognizing a peer amongst the nameless, sweaty strangers.

The mansion had been transformed into a miniature nightclub decked out to the max for this occasion.

I'm not sure his parents would agree, but Troy Sainte had truly outdone himself this year. I'd ask him to help me find my sister, but I knew he'd want something in return, namely a blow job. That wasn't happening. I'd sooner choke on a piece of shit.

With a defeated huff, I turned on my heel and rescanned the room as far as my eye could see. Taking a good look at the crowd, I began to make sense of why Lamia chose to meet here.

When she was thrown out, she was essentially exiled from my life. We weren't supposed to be speaking anymore. This was a perfect place to meet without being spotted by someone on our parents' payroll or looking to kiss some ass.

We were too well known to go anywhere local without risking it getting back to them. I would've agreed to that too, though. She was worth the potential consequences. Unlike the rest of the family, I couldn't just forget her existence. I missed her more with each passing day.

My sister was one of my best friends which is why I assumed she would be eagerly looking for me too. She had to know that I'd be coming with Melantha and Gracelyn. I rarely went anywhere without those two.

Where the hell could she be for her not to have spotted any of us yet? I was starting to grow concerned. Had she left for some reason? We'd been searching a good twenty minutes and she was no longer reading any of my texts

It was too loud in here to call her.

The sheer volume of the music wasn't going to allow for that. I could feel the bass through the tips of my red-bottomed pumps.

Just as I avoided a head-on collision with a girl in a mini skirt, Gracelyn reached out a hand to help me escape the vortex of aggressive twerking I'd almost been sucked into.

"You find Mia?" she leaned in and yelled, damn near destroying my eardrum in her attempt to be heard over the music.

I spared her the same pain and shook my head to indicate I hadn't had any luck. She tapped the red cup in my hand with a perfectly manicured nail. "What's this?"

I shrugged and mouthed back, *"I don't know."*

Her pretty face morphed into a scowl, and she snatched the drink away making me laugh. I hadn't planned on drinking it. I wasn't an idiot.

Some random guy who could've passed as an extra in Blade since he thought it was cool to wear sunglasses indoors had given it to me, saying something about being at a party empty-handed.

I'd been looking for a place to ditch it without having to venture all the way back to the kitchen. Gracelyn simply dumped the contents in a random decorative vase before placing the cup beside a few others that had been abandoned.

I nudged her shoulder to ease us further away from the makeshift dance floor. "Where's, Mel?"

She looped her arm through mine and pointed in the general direction of the patio. I continued to keep an eye out for my sister as we made the short journey to that side of the house. As we were passing the spacious billiard room, I did a quick check to make sure she wasn't with the group of people gathered inside.

I didn't see Lamia, but someone else did catch my eye. *Again.* He was the last person I expected to see here. I'd had both the pleasure and displeasure of falling into our usual routine multiple times since my arrival. He was with his usual crew, plus a few stragglers. I'd heard he and his friends typically stuck to parties that were so private you only knew the location the day of and through a secretive messaging system. I had no clue how true this was or not.

Secrets and mystery were a natural part of the lives we lived, meaning it could be a truth, lie, or a mix of both. That's why I didn't put much stock in the rumor mill. I knew firsthand how hard it was to fact-check the information circulating through it.

He stood beside the pool table with a stick in hand, waiting for his turn to shoot. He glanced away from the game taking place. Our eyes met and a shiver of awareness snaked down my spine.

It didn't matter how many times I saw him. This reaction was something he seemed to exclusively evoke.

My illicit attraction to him was more than skin deep. I wouldn't argue how fine the guy was, though. I'd always thought he was gorgeous. Not in the way the sun was when it shined in a clear blue sky, but more like a thunderstorm in the middle of the night, filling the darkness with fleeting sparks of light.

His eyes were strikingly blue, standing out against his naturally tan skin. It was a similar shade to Gracelyn's whereas mine was more bronze thanks to my mix of Hispanic and Italian genes. Our connection lasted only a few seconds if that. His supple lips pressed firmly together, and he returned his focus to the game going on, causing a strand of his dark brown hair to fall from its resting place.

He'd changed up the cut since I last saw him, leaving it long on top and short on the sides. Not paying any attention to where I was going, I almost walked right into an angled section of the wall. I dodged it at the last second with a tug from Grace.

"I told you to watch out," she admonished with a laugh.

"I was checking for my sister."

"Sure, you were."

"I was," I argued without any real heat.

"Okay, well, I think Lamia's idea is to *blend* with the crowd. Hanging around those guys is exactly the opposite of blending in."

This was true.

Their popularity aside, they weren't the kind of company we would keep. Our families had a whole *Hatfield's and McCoy's* thing going on. I didn't know all the specifics of why or what began such a long-winded feud.

Whatever it was had been the reason for underlying tension between the other families involved in the politics of our world for as long as I could remember.

Sides were chosen, not based on right or wrong but by who they felt would come out on top whenever all was said and done, which was a risky gamble if you asked me. I thought it would be smarter to remain neutral and align yourself with the better opponent when the timing was right.

Secondly, was simply because of them, who they were.

On the surface, they were gorgeous, intelligent, wealthy, and charming when necessary. If you were to peel back all their layers, you would find the inside wasn't nearly as beguiling. Like Pandora's box, you'd see what kind of evil and cunning viciousness could be found in alluring packages.

These attributes were typically bold red flags for girls brought up in a mundane fashion. I couldn't imagine what that would be like, raised safe and secure instead of in a world of bloodshed and power struggles. It made guys like Ciaran a hot commodity, giving me more incentive to stay away from him.

Grace and I found our way outside where a lavish outdoor retreat awaited. The Saintes' massive in-ground pool had been utilized for tonight's festivity. People were simultaneously drinking while swimming naked.

I hoped a few of the guys in there were growers and not showers or they'd be living down that embarrassment for years to come.

Melantha was waiting for us in the only area of the patio that wasn't congested with foot traffic. With her navy blue and pink hair styled in two adorable sailor buns, she was easy to spot.

"Did you find her?" she asked as soon as we were within hearing distance.

"Nope." I popped my lips on the *p*.

Grace turned and looked towards the pool. "I think we've searched this whole place from top to bottom."

I positioned myself between them and leaned against the cement railing that served as a decorative fence around the flagstone.

"Maybe she's on a mattress being bent into an origami."

"That might be true, but it's not helpful," Grace replied with a laugh.

I frowned. "Mia would not go running off for a quickie when she knew we were coming but thank you two *so* much for that visual."

"What else would you expect her to be doing while waiting? She's finally free to shack up with the guy that put a baby in her. They're probably like bunnies right now," Mel retorted.

She made it sound like being exiled from our family was a good thing. I hated to admit that I understood exactly where she was coming from, but my sister had been robbed of everything aside from her first name for daring to fall for a guy my parents didn't choose.

I was far from wholly accepting that she'd been living a secret life without ever confiding in me, but I wasn't angry. If anything, I was hurt. I'd never betray her trust so why did she keep something so monumental all to herself?

I hoped whoever she'd gotten involved with was well enough off to take care of her until she found her feet. I knew she would be fine in the long run. My sister was a strong and intelligent young woman. This wouldn't be enough to douse the flame of her future. Still, I'd feel a lot better after I saw her to confirm this with my own two eyes.

Pulling my cell from the pocket of my romper, I checked to see how we were on time and then tried to call her. I was immediately met with the robotic voice of her message system.

"Her phone isn't on anymore." I drew in a heavy breath, trapping the scent of barbecue, liquor, and pot in my lungs. Slowly exhaling, I slid my cell back into my pocket, contemplating what to do now. "It's a quarter to nine. The movie was two hours and dinner would maybe be another, what? Two if we're pushing it?"

"Maybe we can say we decided to go to a later showing," Gracelyn suggested, fixing her hazel eyes on my face.

I stared at her a beat. "Are...are you being serious?"

She shrugged. "Is that so unrealistic?"

"My mother sniffs out lies faster than a K9 does when cocaine is dangling in front of its face."

"Mine is probably staring into her freaky ass crystal ball watching us right now," Mel joked.

I looked towards where Sainte's backyard became overtaken by trees. Between them was a pathway lined with paper lanterns. Would Mia have gone down there? It didn't make sense to do that when she knew I'd be coming here to meet her. She'd read the initial text I sent back and said she would be waiting. I hope that meant at the house and not in the damn woods.

Grace tucked a strand of blonde hair behind one ear and toed the flagstone with the suede point of her black thigh-high boot.

"What do you think we should do?"

Boisterous laughter erupted from the opposite side of the patio as a few of the people we'd seen in the den came outside. I glanced at them briefly before returning my attention to Grace and Mel.

"I'll do one final sweep upstairs. You two should at least try and enjoy yourselves for a little."

Mel gave me a disapproving stare. "You know we wouldn't do that. Besides, three heads are better than one. We can check the first floor again. She's gotta be around here somewhere."

"Yeah, why don't we meet here in ten?" Grace proposed.

"Okay." I nodded in agreement, offering them a smile of appreciation.

"Lana!" Troy's inebriated voice called out to me as we made our way back across the patio. "Come swim with me beautiful!"

I looked his way and laughed. He was riding a giant unicorn floatie, naked, of course, with a beer in his hand. Someone had better be planning to sanitize or burn all the inflatables these random genitals were rubbing against. Drain the whole damn pool while they were at it because gross.

"So, that's how it is?" Troy pouted when I didn't reply.

I acknowledged his catcall with another smile and nothing more. He immediately moved on to Mel and Grace, who ignored him altogether. Troy couldn't be taken seriously. He was a cutie, having a strong resemblance to a younger David Beckham with a bit more muscle. That was precisely the problem. He used his looks for his benefit.

If you had a pretty face, you were on Sainte's list of future conquests and an open target for his persistent charms.

I felt a different set of eyes watching us as we stepped inside and went our separate ways. I knew who I'd find if I turned my head, which is precisely why I didn't. There was no point in continuing to entertain myself with his attention right now.

By the time I reached the bottom of the staircase, I was thinking I should have asked for twenty minutes instead of ten.

Getting through the mostly intoxicated crowd had been a task in itself. I jogged up the wideset wooden steps, darting around a couple making out near the top.

I envied them for their ability to do that so freely. Hookups were a foreign notion for me and anyone I dated had to be put through the metaphorical ringer. My parents were old-fashioned as hell.

They wanted all 'unions' to lead to marriage yet were hypocritical about the act itself. Getting into an Ivy League would be easier than putting a ring on my finger. The one and only boyfriend I had decided to dump me completely out of the blue a few months ago, pissing off my entire family.

They were more upset than I was. I knew Brian was never going to be my end game, but that did nothing for his fate. If he had a lick of common sense, he'd lay low for a good twelve months if he didn't want the men in my family to annihilate him.

Thinking of my failed relationship reminded me of the reasons why they weren't worth the effort, no matter who it was. I would never have the final say and I really didn't want to go through the process of trial and error all over again. My sister's situation was a great deterrent. Like her, I didn't want my partner to be hand-picked by my parents.

I knew there was a certain way things were done, but I wanted no parts in that. Being single was definitely for the best. I could always try out some sordid one-night stands—live life on the edge.

Shaking off my momentary melancholy, I reached the second level of the house and paused. More than half of the doors were closed. How did I go about checking the rooms?

I knew for a fact that some of these had been open earlier.

I could listen outside each one for signs of fucking or conversation but with the music being so loud I'd have to press my ear to the wood like some kind of perverted creeper.

Deciding the best way to deal with this was to wing it, I headed down the hall. The first door I stopped in front of was utterly silent. I strained to hear any movement or sound. When nothing came from the other side, I kept going.

As I was passing by the entrance to the semi-enclosed balcony, the panoramic view had me pausing again. I'd seen this earlier and hadn't stopped to look.

I couldn't make myself pass it up a second time despite needing to find my sister as soon as humanly possible. The backyard oasis was surrounded by a sprawling lawn touched by autumn and tall trees, blanketed with a dark overhead sky full of stars.

Time seemed to slow as I got lost in the serenity of it. The party raging below became nothing but background noise. I'm not sure how long I stood there staring into the night, wasting precious seconds.

"I didn't expect to see you tonight."

His husky voice nearly sent me jumping out of my skin. Quickly realizing who was right beside me, I turned so that we were facing one another.

"It would be strange if you were expecting anything from me at all," I replied slowly. Why was he up here?

I took a leisurely scan of his body, noting as many details as possible. He was wearing all black, from his shirt to his boots. The color suited him well. His top was fitted to his body and left little to the imagination. The matching sweats should've been outlawed. The outline of his dick was impossible to miss. Have mercy, that was on soft?

Of all the rumors spread about him, his sexual trysts were extra hush-hush. Judging by the glimpse I just got, if he knew what he was doing then I imagined there was very little to complain about. I fought the temptation to take a better look and said the first thing that popped into my head, needing to get my mind out of the gutter.

"Did you abandon your friends?"

"You could say that," he replied with a blatant note of amusement. "How did you end up here?"

I straightened to my full height, which wasn't much compared to his, "I'm looking for my sister, actually. Have you seen her?"

"Not recently."

Did that mean he'd seen her some other time somehow? I wasn't sure how that would be possible given she was supposed to be laying low and he was the last person she needed to be involved with.

He took a slow, open perusal of my body, going from my head of nearly waist-length dark hair, journeying to the swell of my hips and then down to the heels I was deeply regretting having worn.

It wasn't sexual, yet I felt something stir. His studious regard was predatory like he was sizing me up. I didn't feel repulsed by the attention. His eyes swept back towards my face and paused on my lips for three whole seconds before his brilliant blues met my brown.

I wished I knew what he was thinking right then. I held his stare refusing to shrink beneath the weight of it. Just like there were rumors about him and his friends the same went for me and mine. I wasn't sure which ones he believed or didn't, but something told me he could easily figure out the truths from the lies.

"Every time I see you, I'm reminded that pictures never do you any justice. Every time," he repeated quietly.

I faltered at his unexpected compliment. It wasn't a major phenomenon to see photos of me. Anyone active on social media could but I doubted he found my profiles through our rare pool of mutual friends. Ciaran was two or three years older than me.

He suddenly smiled, showing off teeth so ridiculously perfect that a dentist would weep tears of joy at the sight of them. "I'm not stalking you online."

"I know..."

"I'm inclined to keep up with the news of the company and sometimes you're included, although it has been rarer the last few years."

Of course, that's how he saw pictures of me. I felt like an idiot for not assuming that was the case straight away.

The reason for me not being pictured alongside my family as of late was because they felt the need to keep me more sheltered than usual from the happenings of our screwed-up little world.

Standing here talking to him was an unexpected turn of events I wouldn't forget anytime soon. Ciaran was someone I spent more time avoiding than anything. Him approaching me would never be something he'd do out of sheer friendliness or curiosity.

"So, did you come all the way upstairs to tell me I'm pretty?"

"When did I say you were pretty?"

It donned on me then that he'd never said such a word *officially*. My face heated with embarrassment for possibly the fourth time in my life. It was irritating. I wasn't a girl who blushed or fluttered her lashes because of a pretty boy.

He grinned and gave a slight shake of his head "I was joking, Liliana."

"No need to backtrack on my behalf."

Taking notice of the obvious discomfort I was failing to mask, his smile faded, and he stepped a fraction closer. Fragranced notes of cinnamon and mint danced in the space left between us, his cologne overpowering the scent of my coco butter and Chanel.

"I'm not a person that gives unnecessary flattery. I didn't call you pretty because the word is too weak of an adjective. You're much more than that."

The sincerity in his voice floored me. "Okay, did someone dare you to do this?" I looked around him to see if anyone was lurking nearby.

"I'm beyond the party version of truth or dare," he replied with a touch of amusement. "I really did want to know why you're here."

"I already told—." I stopped myself short, deciding against mentioning Lamia a second time. "I was invited. Is that okay with you?"

"I'm not in a position to have any say in what you do or don't do yet."

"*Yet?*" I eyed him with slightly narrowed eyes. "Did you by chance do drugs tonight?"

His lips twitched as if he were trying not to laugh. "I thought you liked having my undivided attention."

The tempo of my heart picked up speed. I made sure to breathe evenly as I replied. "I wasn't aware that I did."

"Weren't you?"

Was he was being playful? I couldn't get a good enough read on him to say for sure.

I wasn't prepared to deal with him right now. My cell vibrated against my hip, giving me a valid reason to break the weird connection between us. I opened the new group chat notification and saw Grace had dropped a text with her pinned location.

Found her. Need your help.

Okay, that didn't exactly warrant any feelings of relief.

What would they need help for? Was Lamia wasted? No, she would never drink while pregnant. Unless... Nope, wasn't going there. Maybe she was having a moment that required emotional intervention?

They wouldn't need my assistance for that. Grace was far better at handling those kinds of situations. *Shit.* Mel was there too, though. She'd only make it worse. She never softened the edges of her dagger-like tongue for anyone. I read the message twice more before clicking the location link.

Realizing who was still right in front of me watching this all happen without saying a word, I left the map pulled up, and slid my cell back into my pocket.

"So...this little chat has been super random. Next time we speak let's pretend it never happened."

I went to step around him and immediately found my path blocked. Now even closer than before, I had to tilt my head back so that I could still see his face. "What are you doing?"

"I'm sorry," he apologized, "I didn't come up here to scare you."

Laughing lightly, I took a step away from him. "I'm not scared of you."

"Good. Remember that."

"I just said we *shouldn't* remember this."

His head tilted slightly to the side. "So, you still won't be talking to me then?"

"Okay, I'm really..." *Oh.*

My sluggish brain finally understood his question. That *undivided attention* comment didn't seem so far out of left field now. The knowing glint in his eyes clued me in that he was aware it'd all just clicked for me.

He and I encountered each other multiple times at various events alongside our families, but we'd never officially met.

There were no grand introductions but more of a hand gesture with muttered honorifics. My parents were good at making nice with people they didn't like, but over the past year or so tension between his family and those closest to them family had gotten so bad they didn't even try anymore.

What they didn't know was that Ciaran and I had an unnerving magnetic pull to one another we refused to act on. Neither of us had ever allowed ourselves to be drawn in too close.

Ciaran would occasionally watch me from afar and I sometimes watched him back.

It was a subtle game of cat and mouse. There wasn't an opportunity to speak freely. We both did a good job of making sure there wasn't a situation where we'd be tempted to. Too many eyes watched our every move as if anticipating the day our dynamic would change.

We always wound up doing the same song and dance, two sharks making figure eights in blood-infested waters, purposely remaining out of reach from one another. It was a dangerously unorthodox relationship we'd developed, but neither seemed inclined to end it.

Whatever his reason was for speaking to me all of a sudden and breaching a barrier I thought we'd established would have to remain a mystery. I couldn't stand around playing twenty-one questions to figure it out. I peered up at him and ignored the voice in my head telling me to get closer.

"I guess I'll keep this in mind then," I responded with a pep I didn't feel.

He stepped out of the way to let me pass, throwing one last curveball at me. "You'll say goodbye before you go?"

"Maybe." I tossed him a smile and walked away. I swear he laughed, but I refused to look back.

I needed to find Lamia and leave. I kept my pace natural and confident, eyes trained straight ahead. I felt his stare on my back the entire way down the hall.

Only when I reached the bottom of the staircase did I feel like I could breathe freely again. All the sounds that had faded into the background surrounded me once more now that I'd escaped the dark orbit, he'd pulled me into. The delayed sensations now spiraling through my chest had nothing to do with me being afraid. I'd been telling the truth about that.

Though, in this scenario that might do me some good.

Sometimes fear wasn't a bad thing. It was natural and under the right circumstances kept people alive. What I was feeling now was *much* worse. I was far too curious for my own good, captivated by someone that was not only bad for me but off-limits.

I was on a path I had to carefully navigate if I had any chance in hell of being free of the chains my family had me in. I needed to stay focused and away from everything that tempted me to stray. Ciaran Belair was at the top of my list.

CHAPTER TWO

Despite the path between the trees being mostly clear of leaves and lit by softly glowing lights, I didn't think we were supposed to go into the woods. No-one stopped me or asked what I was doing when I came this way, though.

The party was in full swing a few yards behind me while straight ahead was nothing, but a trail of dancing shadows wrapped in silence. If the circumstances were different, I would have found this as serene as the upstairs view. Who didn't love a good evening stroll through nature?

According to my phone's GPS, Grace and Mel had definitely come this way and wherever they'd gone was somewhere along this trail.

I hit the call button and listened to the sound of ringing until I was greeted by an automated voicemail.

This was weird.

Grace's pin remaining stationary was enough to kick my ass into gear, moving at a pace that was sustainable in heels. The air grew cooler the further I went into the woods, carrying a tincture of earthiness. Loose leaves gathered at my feet, a few twigs peppered among them.

I rounded a small bend, crossing my arms while keeping my cell's flashlight aimed in front of me. The outline of two people began to take shape in the distance, coming from the opposite direction. As we grew closer to one another I was able to see the way they were dressed.

I slowed, muttering, "What the fuck?"

"Don't be afraid," the girl called to me softly.

Said like a true serial killer, I thought bemusedly. The guy with her resembled Twisty the clown and the dark-haired girl at his side was some kind of jester. This made three people now that were wearing costumes when Halloween was nearly four months away.

Seeing they lacked concern or panic made me feel marginally better. If something serious was wrong, I assumed they'd know. Once we were practically shoulder to shoulder, I stopped so that I could ask if they had seen my friends

The jester eyed my outfit with a pout. "You're not in the right clothes."

She sounded legitimately disappointed I wasn't wearing a costume like she was. Instead of pointing out the obvious, I pretended I forgot. "Oh, I wasn't planning to come. It was a last-minute thing. Did either of you happen to see a group of girls back there?"

A grin that came off more sly than friendly split her face in two. "They've been waiting for you."

What the fuck? I shifted my gaze from her to the clown whose unsettling stare was burning holes into my face. "Are they okay?"

Her toothy grin melted into a closed-mouth smile. With the slightest shrug of her shoulders, she replied with a carefree, "Sure."

She and the clown walked away then, leaving me to stare at their retreating forms.

"Thanks for your help."

"Have fun," she sang softly in return.

What was going on with the people at this party? I turned away and resumed my trek. After three or four more minutes I spotted an opening in the trees a few feet ahead. Grace's dot still remained in the same location while mine continued to grow closer.

My signal was steadily depleting, but at least I knew that this was the right direction. I reached the end of the path and came to a dead stop, double-checking my phone to confirm what I already knew would be the case.

"Oh, *fuck* no."

I hit call on Grace's number and got voicemail again. I tried Mel next, but her line rang until I got the same thing. Lamia's phone was still off. Grace had texted me and I could still her location. She would need to be in range for that. So why wasn't she answering the damn phone? I was beginning to have a bad feeling about this.

I eyed the gated wooden arch that served as an entrance to a cornfield I wasn't aware existed. Lantern lights had been wrapped around the thick wooden pillars that connected to a tall mesh fence. A large scarecrow with a glowing head was to the immediate right of the entryway.

This field wasn't visible from the upper level of Sainte's home. I wasn't really sure why this was here at all. Did his parents grow corn as a hobby? I scanned the stalks, straining to hear voices, and picked up on a steady stream of music coming from somewhere beyond what I could see.

"Have to be fucking kidding me," I muttered. Were they partying back here too? At this point, I wanted to say the night couldn't get any more bizarre and off track, but I wasn't going to hold my breath on that.

My common sense was screaming not to go into this goddamn field, but I didn't have much of a choice. Absolute worst-case scenario I'd run into some masked assholes trying to play *Children of The Corn*. I could handle that.

I stepped through the wooden arch, adding the sole inscription at the very top to memory so I could decipher it later.

Making my way through the field itself wasn't too bad, wearing the wrong footwear aside. The cornstalks were taller than me and cut my view off from everything else, but the path between them was wide and clear-cut.

I was pleasantly surprised at how good they smelled. They had a lush and rich aroma, with a hint of honey and something floral. After I took a few more predetermined turns a building began to take shape and the sound of music grew louder, the voice of my man Ozzy becoming clearer. Finally, another arch signified the exit point I needed to cross through.

That gut instinct to go back was twice as strong now. Intuition began to hit me with warning signals demanding I turn my ass around. Continuing went against every bit of common sense I possessed, a giant middle finger to everything I'd been taught growing up.

I couldn't stop now. I was damn near on top of where Grace and Mel should be. I passed through the exit and found myself staring up at a large wooden barn where the music was coming from at a near-deafening volume. I officially felt like those infuriatingly idiotic girls that made all the wrong choices in horror movies, except this was real.

I calmed my vivid imaginings with facts.

No one had been hiding in the cornfield and there wasn't going to be a psycho wielding a chainsaw coming at me from inside this barn.

Being cautious for self-preservation's sake, I slowly approached the large structure. I noticed right away that it didn't have any of the luxury fixtures or elements I'd expect from a Sainte property. In fact, it looked rather dull and plain sitting in the center of a leveled dirt circle.

There were no windows or notable features apart from a large set of matching pine doors. My attention was drawn to the large black bar keeping them closed. I silently cursed at the sight of it. Did someone lock Grace and Mel inside? What a dick move.

I knocked on the door to see if I'd get a response. When I didn't, I slid my phone back into my pocket so that I could use both hands to grab the round metal handle. It didn't budge an inch at first. I tightened my grip and with a grunt, I pulled hard to the left. With a loud clang, the heavy bar slid out of place. The sudden momentum nearly knocked me on my ass.

Both doors swung open to reveal a metal grate going from floor to ceiling a few inches inside the doorway.

Mel, Grace, and a couple people I wasn't familiar with were all on the other side of it. My sister was nowhere in sight.

"Lana?" Mel questioned with a hint of confusion when she realized who had opened the barn. I stepped inside intending to let everyone out. A guy in the back yelled out for me to stop.

His warning came a fraction of a second too late. Once I passed over the threshold, both barn doors slammed shut and the metal grate immediately retracted. Looking up at the high ceiling, I spotted a track-like pulley system that had been triggered.

A loud bang echoed from behind me, a sign the bar I'd just removed had slid back into place. The music abruptly cut off, leaving heavy breathing to fill the cutting silence.

"Did you see that? Fuck, we're never getting out of here!" A curvy blonde yelled.

Grace rushed towards me and grabbed hold of my shoulders, checking my body over from top to bottom. "Are you okay?"

"I'm fine." I took hold of her hands and gently removed them. "What is going on?"

"How did you find us?" Mel asked, coming to stand beside Grace.

"I got your location in a text from Grace that said you needed help. Not that I did you much good."

Grace shook her head back and forth. "Lana, I never text you."

"Well, someone did."

I pulled my cell from my pocket and showed her the screen I still had pulled up on the *Find My* app. Her dot was showing right where we both were. They shared a look before settling their gazes on me. I didn't like what I saw. Mel's silver eyes had darkened and there was a pensive expression marring her porcelain features.

"They lured her here too," a heavily accented voice carried from the far side of the barn.

"What is she talking about?"

Grace expelled a breath and glanced at my screen again. "I left my phone in the car because I thought we'd be in and out."

I didn't know that. Hadn't I locked my doors? Come to think of it, where were my keys? I ran my hands over both pockets and realized my fob was gone. I did it again to make sure I wasn't tripping. Where the hell did my keys go?

"What is happening? Someone got into my car and stole your cellphone to trick me into coming here? How would they know you even left it there?"

"Because they're clearly on bullshit," Mel seethed. "Do you know how we got here? Some bitch dressed as a clown told us L would meet us in the barn. It made sense at the moment.

"Now that I'm in here I feel like a fucking idiot for walking through those doors."

"That makes two of us. I think I know who you're talking about."

I looked towards the other people inside with them. "How did everyone else get shut in here? Don't tell me you all went waltzing through a cornfield together."

"Kind-of. I was coming to score some shrooms from my buddy," a guy with long black hair answered.

Lovely. I'm pretty sure we had chemistry together my sophomore year because he'd been held back for skipping the class so many times two years before.

"So, someone made sure that all…" I trailed off and counted how many people were inside the barn. There was the curvy blonde. She probably had people looking for her. There was a tall brunette wearing some type of chic cultural dress. A guy with glasses, a redhead, and another dude with a man-bun.

"Eight of us got locked in. Does anyone know why?" Multiple looks were exchanged, but no one seemed to have an answer.

"Do any of you have someone else at the party we can call?"

"You can't use your phone inside here," the guy with glasses answered. His dark eyes peered at me from behind their thin rims.

"Why not?" I checked my network bars and saw he was right. The same cellphone that got me all the way here no longer had a signal and had gone into 'searching' on the app.

I laughed despite nothing about this situation being remotely funny. Was I dreaming right now?

"Someone's using a jammer. They let the phones work off and on." Glasses held his phone up for me to see we had the same issue. "We were sent to get more beer." He motioned towards the dude with the man-bun.

I belatedly realized their shirts correlated.

The revelation that they walked through a cornfield in the middle of the night for beer they'd have to carry all the way back to the house when there were already cases of it stacked all over the place could only mean one thing.

"You're pledging?"

"*Kappa Azathoth*," his friend cupped his hands over his mouth and hollered in a theatrically deep voice.

"I have officially entered hell," Mel mumbled.

Azathoth? These two were connected to the same circle as us then. That frat belonged to Apollon University, which meant they were ridiculously gifted in some type of academic field to be attending there in the first place.

"I'm Dion, that's Max," he put forward.

I nodded and forwent doing the same. In any other circumstance, I would've loved to sit and pick his brain, right now we needed to figure out how we were going to get out of here.

"Unless the plan was to lock us away to die, there has to be something inside this barn that will help us get out."

"Yeah, because we didn't think of any of this shit already, newbie," the guy with long hair retorted sarcastically. He made it sound as if they were an exclusive clique I'd requested to join.

Mel turned on him with a glare. "Look at that, the guy who was damn near crying in the corner has suddenly decided to dig deep within himself and find his tiny little balls. Maybe you should thank her for helping you with that."

"Hey. It's fine, he's no one," I said softly.

Despite him saying they already had, I searched the room anyways with fresh eyes. It was close to empty. There were a few bales of hay stacked in a corner people had turned into seats.

An old car was parked off to the left. A heavy-duty tool bench was to the right. Another set of doors was on the back wall but seeing as they'd all been stuck in here longer than I had it was safe to assume they were locked too. My attention slowly drifted back to the dusty Station Wagon. It didn't fit in. Everything around us looked new, including the plain-looking building itself.

"That shouldn't be here."

"Cooper just checked it and said there wasn't anything inside," Dion replied, implicating the guy with long hair.

"I'll check it again then, just in case."

"You do that sweetheart, kill some time," he responded with a forced laugh.

I ignored his petty sarcasm and walked over to the car, yanking open the driver's side door, causing the hinges to groan in loud protest. I stuck my head inside and was immediately smacked with a smell that reminded me of eraser dust.

All the leather was cracked and had foam spilling out.

"I'll re-check the back," Grace volunteered. She climbed into the rear seat and began to diligently look over the faded yellow and cream exterior.

I opened the glove compartment and then ran my hands over the ruined seats. It was the passenger one where my palms skimmed across something hard. I pressed down lightly and felt the outline of a rectangular object.

"Did you find something?" Mel asked in a whisper, watching over my shoulder.

"Maybe..." I didn't want to say for sure until I saw what it was. There was no point in getting everyone excited over nothing. Slipping my fingers beneath the torn leather, I started to pull and pluck.

Chunks of yellow foam fell to the floor as I burrowed deeper into the inner workings of the bucket seat.

The tips of my coffin nails scraped against something plastic. Wrinkling my nose, I stretched my fingers as far as I could until I had three wrapped around the object good enough to start pulling. After a few back-and-forth motions, I tugged it free.

"Seriously?"

Grace stopped what she was doing and peered between the seats with a frown. "Someone's really taking this prank gig to heart."

Mel peeked over my shoulder and cursed when she saw what was in my hand. "Who the fuck still uses those?"

"The police?" I shuffled backward and placed my aching feet back on the dirt floor of the barn.

"I don't think they had much to do with this," Grace remarked.

"What is that?" Max questioned when he looked at my hand.

"It's a tape recorder," the blonde voiced loud enough for everyone to hear. "How did you miss that when *you* searched the car before?" she lobbied at Cooper.

"I must've overlooked it, sorry. It's just a tape deck. How is it going to help?"

I flipped the recorder towards the small circle everyone had started to form around me. The brunette's brows furrowed as she read the message someone had scribbled on the black device in red ink. "*Play with me?*"

"You're not actually going to listen to that, are you?" Dion asked. He eyed the device from behind his thin-rimmed glasses as if it were the devil itself.

"I don't see why we wouldn't," Mel replied. "There's a tape inside, isn't there?"

Her question was rhetorical, but I answered anyway. "Yeah, and it was probably here for a reason." I don't know if I said that more for them or myself, but this felt like the right course of action.

It wasn't like we had anything better to do or a ton of other options. We were trapped inside a barn and none of our cellphones worked. Finding this tape was not a coincidence. Someone had diligently done the groundwork in anticipation of it being found. Despite the voice in my head starting to stir up doubts again, I took a breath and pressed play.

CHAPTER THREE

At first, there was nothing but the sound of the tape spinning. When someone finally began to speak, their voice gave off a discomforting Loli vibe. It sounded almost exactly like the jester from back in the woods.

"*It's my favorite time of year and what better way to celebrate than with a group of special friends?*" she trilled happily.

"What a nutcase," the ninja mumbled.

"*Now, I've got a few secrets you'll be dying for me to share, but first we're going to see who amongst you deserves to hear it.*" At the end of her sentence, a portion of wood paneling above the tool bench slid up.

There were mixed reactions as a variety of masks affixed to the wall and a small digital clock were revealed.

"Surprise! I got you all a present. Hurry over and put on your new faces. I'll give you four minutes to get yourselves ready!"

"Is this real?" the blonde stammered, wringing her hands together.

I didn't know how to answer that. Clearly, someone had gone through the trouble of setting all this up. It was pretty elaborate and well thought out for a prank, but also impressive.

"I'm annoyed with how intrigued I am right now," Mel quietly divulged.

"Me too."

Despite the given situation, I wanted to see how everything would pan out. Keeping hold of the recorder, I walked over to the tool bench with Mel and Grace to get a better look at the clock and masks. Dion followed right behind us.

"They have our names beneath them," Grace pointed out.

I looked over each mask, seeing they were all different except for our three that were the same style of LED in different colors.

"Here." Mel stretched up and grabbed two of the three off the wall. She handed Grace the pink one and me the white, removing the blue assigned to her last.

"Y'all are *wearing* those?" Cooper asked, sounding completely baffled by our decision.

Mel smiled at him as she slid her mask on. "They want to play a game, right? I say let's play."

"Yes, let us see what will happen." The brunette made her way to the front of the group. "Can someone hand me mine? It's, Hayven."

"You're the bunny."

Grace placed her mask on her head and then snagged the leather piece with rabbit ears down.

"Anyone else?" Mel asked.

They looked at us as if we'd lost our minds. I placed my mask on and bit my lower lip to smother a laugh. It was lightweight and breathable, allowing me to see out perfectly. I didn't get what they were all so afraid of. We were here now, and my night was already ruined. I didn't see the point in wallowing.

I should've been in a cozy theater right about now, thinking ahead to the meal I'd order at my favorite bar and restaurant. My ETA home was going to be blown to shit. I hadn't met my sister and unless this wrapped up quickly I probably wouldn't.

Whoever was fucking with us was partially responsible for everything that had gone wrong.

The voice on the recording came back, gaining everyone's attention.

"Time's up! I hope you all prepared well. I'll be mighty disappointed if you let me down.

Now listen closely, it's a matter of life and death.

Sixteen in total, take away one.

The price to be paid is within your hands.

A small token to show you're paying attention.

Your ears will hear.

The mind will solve.

Your tongue will help you give me what I want.

Once you see it, take a breath.

One quick cut and the maze awaits.

Be quick and steadfast, you have fifteen minutes. If you fail, your life is forfeit.

Tick, tock, it's time for judgement."

There was an audible click that signaled the recording had ended.

"What did she mean by *our lives will be forfeit?*" Max questions, his voice slightly shaking.

"Who knows. It's nothing to be scared about. All of this is clearly some big ass ruse to make us shit our pants," Cooper replied.

"I think we should try to solve the riddle in case it is more than that," Hayven argued.

He rolled his eyes and stepped away from the tool bench. "Suit yourselves. I'm going to sit down until the clock hits zero. They should let us out afterward."

I glanced down and saw a countdown of sorts had begun. Based on the numbers already shown it had started as soon as the recording ended.

How was that possible? Someone had to be listening in or watching us right this second. That was the only logical explanation for the way everything was panning out.

"I don't think they're going to just let us go. Think about it, why go through all the trouble of setting this up just to open the doors anyways?"

He didn't respond, but he didn't flat-out reject my theory either.

"That makes sense," Dion agreed.

"*Or* like Cooper said, whoever is doing this only wants to scare us," the redhead suddenly chimed in. There was a hint of southern twang in her tone. "Why would we feed into this crap? Do you really believe we'll be in real-life danger for not going along with some weird kids' elaborate prank?"

Well, there she and I had a difference of opinion. If this person was a kid, then technically so were we and I didn't think they were weird. I thought they were kind of brilliant. I didn't say any of this out loud. I could sense a debate brewing and knew to diffuse any possibility of it beginning.

This may have been some ridiculous scheme thought up by who knows, but I'd decided to play along and right now every second wasted was one we couldn't get back.

"We have approximately thirteen minutes left to solve this riddle. How about focusing on that so we have a better chance of possibly getting out of here?"

"Wait. Shouldn't we introduce ourselves first?"

I looked towards Cooper with slightly raised brows. "Is that direly important right now?"

"In the future when you tell your grandkids how you got locked in a barn with a group of strangers, won't you want to tell them their names?"

The answer to that was a simple no. I didn't plan on having children so there would be no possibility of grandkids, but I didn't need to tell him any of that.

I also refrained from pointing out his lack of awareness of our surroundings. Less than a foot away two masks belonged to the girls not wearing them.

"Which one of you is Elizabeth"

"Me," the blonde raised her hand.

"Then that makes her Jessica." I pointed to the redhead. "Now we're all introduced."

"Too good to tell us who you are?" he challenged.

I forced a smile while reigning in my temper. He was testing my patience and when that was gone, he was going to profusely regret speaking to me at all.

"Can you stop? Everyone knows who they are, man. Knock it off," Dion cut in.

Mm. Brownie points for him.

"She mentioned sixteen..." Grace trailed off, voicing her thoughts out loud.

"Isn't fifteen the answer then? We have to take away one, right?" Elizabeth speculated.

Mel was quick to shoot her down. "No. That's far too simple."

I repeated the riddle as best as I could inside my head and found myself studying my hands. "Are we supposed to touch something? Maybe grab onto something? I don't know what else could be in here we need to see."

"Within our grasp...I think you're on the right track," Max replied animatedly.

"What if it's senses then?" Mel suggested.

Dion made a sound of agreement and nodded. "You're both right."

"Then what is the answer?" Jessica prodded with audible irritation in her tone.

"Use that beautiful brain of yours to help figure it out," Cooper taunted in a flirtatious manner.

She flicked him off and turned to face the opposite direction.

"The missing sense would be touch," I stated. "In the...riddle if that's what we're calling it, she named four. We see. Hear. Taste and smell. Wait, no. It can't be senses. The mind part doesn't fit."

"It might not be about the senses exactly, but they're definitely part of it," Max countered.

"Okay, then we need to figure out how that's going to help get these doors open."

"I'm going to check the car again." Mel declared.

"I'll help," Dion quickly volunteered, following on her heels with Hayven in tow.

"Wanna check the wall?" Cooper looked to me and asked, his arrogance suddenly non-existent.

"Yeah, let's do that." I didn't like him at all, but I wouldn't let my personal feelings get in the way of figuring this out.

Grace walked with us to where the panel had lifted and stood to the side.

Cooper went up to the worktable and slightly leaned forward to inspect the gap that had formed between the wall and tool bench.

"Is there anything specific I should be looking for?"

"Whatever doesn't look right, I guess."

"Can you get my mask down?" Elizabeth asked as she approached with Max. "Maybe that will change something."

"Worth a try." I reached up and snagged each one that had been left hanging, passing Elizabeth hers.

To our mutual frustration, nothing happened. Nothing was happening and a glance at the clock showed we had less than eight minutes left to change that. My competitive nature refused to accept losing.

"This is maddening," Grace huffed. "I feel like the answer is *right* in front of our faces."

"It could be. That might be the point of the riddle. Can I see that?" Max held his hand out for his off-white mask.

Unsure what he meant, I passed it to him. He slipped it on before stepping around us and joining Cooper in examining the rectangular hole that had been formed as a result of the wall opening up.

"Sixteen in total," he murmured to himself, running his palms around the frame. "Look, there's a groove here."

Grace and I both moved to get a closer look at what he was referring to, watching Max trace over a barely noticeable u-shaped curve in the bottom portion of the wood.

"I think there might be something down in there." He reached through the opening, his shoulder pressing up against the wall as he worked his hand down into the gap.

"You guys find anything?" Mel called from across the barn.

"Not yet." I looked over my shoulder to find they were quite literally tearing the car apart. The driver's side door panel was hanging on by a single screw.

"Woah!" Cooper shouted.

My head swiveled around just as the portion of the wall that had lifted up, came crashing back down, right on top of where Max's wrist ended. He released a short disbelieving laugh as the color drained from his face.

Before anyone could ask if he was okay or make a move to help free him, his mouth opened with a guttural scream of pain. I flinched and stepped away from him, taking Grace with me.

"What happened?" Jessica ran towards us with a worried cry.

The clock blanked to zero, and the panel lifted again, revealing a butcher-like blade embedded in the wood. Had that been in there the entire time?

Max went spiraling backward. I blinked at the sight of him cradling the stump that his hand should have been attached to.

"Oh, fuck," Cooper quavered, turning away with dry heaves wracking his body.

I looked from Max to the opening in the wall where a part of his severed hand could still be seen. There was so much blood. It covered the tool bench and the floor, spilling out of him in a dangerously incessant flow.

Elizabeth lost her shit. She ran screaming incoherently towards a set of doors shouting to let us out.

"What the fuck?" Mel mouthed as she approached, her eyes locked on Max.

Dion raced over and dropped to his knees beside his friend. "Why would you put your hand in there and you didn't even know what it was?" He pulled off his T-shirt and began to make a tourniquet, staining the life-beater beneath with his friend's blood.

"Cheers to you! You've all passed the first test. Get ready now, the real fun is about to begin."

At the sound of her voice, panic began to grip the rest of the people inside the barn. I did my best to block out the negative energy they were emanating and focus on everything around me. Her voice definitely wasn't coming from the tape recorder now. My eyes darted around in search of a speaker or camera.

"Let us out, you crazy fucking bitch!" Jessica yelled.

She giggled at the insult and sighed. *"I'm so excited you're ready to play. Show us you have what it takes to survive in the place where sinners play."*

The sound of the metal bar finally sliding back echoed throughout the barn, but it wasn't the doors I walked through that unlocked.

The pair Elizabeth was banging on opened, causing her to pitch forward and fall right into the person waiting on the other side as they swung outward. Her gasp was drowned out by Jessica's terrified scream as someone donning a bloodied fox mask knocked Elizabeth backward.

She hit the ground and stared up at the person cocking their head to the side as they looked down at her.

"Please don't. I'm sorry, I'll never do it again."

Her plea had me wondering if she knew this person. It didn't seem to matter if that were the case. Without uttering a word, the man stepped forward and raised the ax.

CHAPTER FOUR

The blade lodged in the center of her face. A crack that reminded me of an egg being broken preceded pure chaos. The music started to play again, cloaking the screams and shouting that erupted.

The three of us helped Dion get Max on his feet as everyone else ran for the exit. We veered left while they went right, keeping as much space as possible between us and the man crushing Elizabeth's chest with a solid black boot as he removed his ax from her face. Her body folded to the ground, a gaping split revealing bone tissue and muscle. She was still twitching when I took my final look at her.

The back of the barn was surrounded by more stalks that lined a dirt path. Simple geography was enough to know it would be leading us away from the maze that brought us all here, but there was no time to stop and debate what to do. Another masked figure came around the corner, forcing us to either keep moving or face off with them and the ax-wielding psychopath.

Dion held onto Max and propelled him forward. I cursed and kicked my heels off, running alongside Grace and Mel. The path curved off to the right. We followed the bend until we came upon a small clearing that split into a T. Despite reaching this point before us, the others were here still, waiting like mindless sheep.

A scarecrow had been placed here for this occasion. Arrows hung from each of its arms, one pointing left and the other right, painted red with *life* or *death*.

It was plain to see whichever route you chose would be leading you right into the woods that lacked any traces of light.

"Which way?" Max rasped.

His breathing was labored, the run causing more harm to his already weakened state. Things were looking grim for him, and I had a feeling we weren't done running yet. The shirt Dion used as a tourniquet was saturated already. If we didn't get him help soon, he would bleed out.

"How do we find the way out of here?" Jessica asked, worriedly glancing over her shoulder.

"We already know the way out. The gate is in the opposite direction," Mel reminded her.

The sound of laughter and taunting catcalls carried from somewhere within the cornfield. The stalks were so high it was impossible to pinpoint where they were coming from.

Dion readjusted his hold on Max and moved him a few inches away from the husks. "We're sitting ducks right here. We gotta keep going."

"What's the move? Death?" Grace asked me as if I held the answers for our salvation.

With a nod, I swallowed and glanced between the two arrows. "Life is logical and easy. We need death."

Jessica made a sound of disagreement and stepped in the opposite direction. "How do you know that's not what they *want* us to believe?"

"I obviously fucking don't."

A body crashing through the stalks with enough momentum to cause a wave-like effect interrupted our ill-timed debate. We came together in a huddle, all eyes trained on different sections of the cornfield.

More than one person was lurking in the stalks. They made it impossible to tell where.

A few mere feet away, the clown I'd crossed paths with earlier burst into the clearing with something clutched in his frilly gloved hands. Jessica whimpered loudly at the sight of him, a violent shudder causing her to sway on her feet.

The clown grinned as he slowly let a chain unravel into a lasso of sorts. Tiny pieces of spiked metal were woven between the links. He began to twirl it in the air, sending the loop towards our huddle after it had gained enough speed to make a whizzing noise.

Jessica screeched so loud I reflexively shoved her away from my ear. My push had her bumping into Cooper, saving him from having his head roped like livestock. The clown laughed at his miss and lunged forward. Mel was forced away from us to keep herself out of his reach, getting swept away by everyone else's terror.

Jessica practically climbed on her back as she ran away. Cooper was the only one that charged in the opposite direction, knocking me down in the process. His shoulder slammed into mine and sent me to the ground with a hard thud.

Grace grabbed hold of my wrist and all but dragged me away before I could attempt to get back on my feet. Once I finally managed to get my legs beneath me, we entered the woods.

"Mel went the other way," I breathed, grimacing as twigs and leaves bit into the soles of my feet.

"Yeah, she had to." Hearing the evident worry in her voice, I gently freed myself from her hold and focused on trying to see where I was going. There were no more lanterns. Our only light came from the masks we had yet to remove, a faint glow of pink and white.

"We need to go back," Cooper stressed.

"You can do whatever you want," I replied evenly.

I knew the guy was an asshole from the second he opened his mouth but knocking me down and then running away without attempting to help me get back up was the ultimate dick move. I was all for self-preservation and I still wouldn't have done the same to him if the situation was reversed. I even would've helped Jessica if it was necessary.

Now I had zero regard for his well-being. All *I* needed to do was find Mel and get us the hell out of here. I mentally mapped the layout of Sainte's house and the woods behind it. I wasn't going exploring in the dark when people were trying to hunt us down. We needed to make our way back to the barn somehow and then through the corn maze without being caught by whoever was after us.

"What if we--?"

Grace abruptly turned and placed her hand over the mouthpart of my mask "Did you hear that?" she whispered.

I shook my head and listened for whatever had caught her attention.

"There's nothing there."

"*Shut up,*" she hissed at Cooper.

He ignored her warning and kept going. "But there will be if we don't find our way out of the woods. We should have gone with the others."

I turned my head, focusing on a patch of darkness up ahead as the sound of footsteps finally reached me. I tugged on Grace's wrist and took a step back, turning towards where it was coming from. As it grew louder, closer, it became clear that whoever was on their way to where we were didn't care if we heard them or not. To know almost exactly where we'd wound up was telling.

"We can't stay on this path," I murmured.

I turned and peered down the hill on our immediate left. It was spotted with trees and overgrown weeds, but it looked to level out after a few feet.

"You want to go *into* the woods?" Cooper shrilled loudly.

Grace growled in annoyance and tossed her head to look at him. "Have you looked around to see where we're at?"

I ignored his presence and focused on my best friend. "If we keep going in the direction these paths take us, they'll know exactly where we are at every turn."

"We're lambs heading towards slaughter," Grace agreed solemnly.

An anguished scream tore through the air, sending a shiver of apprehension down my spine.

"Come on." I grabbed Grace's hand and we stepped off the poorly maintained path. I did my best to watch where I stepped.

Max's hand had been severed by him triggering something. I didn't want to do the same and cost me or Gracelyn a limb. Cooper cursed loudly and began to follow us down the uneven slope. Our descent was slow, our masks not bright enough to light more than what was barely right in front of our faces. My feet smushed into greenery and dirt. I grimaced when something tiny with legs scuffled over my toes.

We were close to what I hoped would be the bottom when Cooper's dumbass tripped. I heard his body pitch forward and come tumbling down. Grace was torn away from me within the blink of an eye. I tried to hold onto her and remain upright, reaching for the trunk of a tree, but failing spectacularly.

"*Fuck*," I hissed as one of my nails broke off entirely and another cracked, causing me to lose my grip. I slid the rest of the way down the slope, knocking the air from my lungs.

When I landed at the bottom in a mess of leaves, twigs, and scratched limbs, I laid completely still for a second trying to get my bearings back. The sound of a struggle a few feet away had me rolling onto my stomach and pushing myself into a standing position.

I couldn't immediately make out what was happening. I could see that Grace was beneath Cooper. For a split second, I thought he may have landed that way, but then I saw the glint of a blade.

"Get off me!" Grace growled, managing to deck him with a well-placed hit.

The sound of her fist hitting his flesh, and a painful grunt spurred me into action. I ate the distance between us and throwing my weight into it, I shoved him with both hands. It was enough to dislodge him entirely.

"What the fuck are you doing?" I grabbed for Grace and helped her stand.

Cooper came at us brandishing the knife, I shoved her out of the way and turned to protect my face and throat as he swung, pulling my lower lip between my teeth to smother a cry of pain as my upper arm was sliced open. I felt blood well and start leaking from the cut. I fought the reflexive urge to touch it, cognizant of how filthy my hands were.

"Have you lost your goddamn mind?" Grace ran forward and grabbed the wrist he was using to wield the knife before he could take another jab at me.

"You weren't supposed to figure it out," he yelled back at her, using his body mass to try and throw her off. Like a dog with a bone, she refused to let go.

I went wide and jumped him from behind. I kicked the back of his leg with the heel of my foot and served his head another hit with my fist.

He folded onto one leg followed by the other when Grace slammed her knee into his face. There was a satisfying crunch and bellow of pain. The knife fell from his hand, and I hopped over him to snag it off the ground, nearly falling onto my face when he grabbed my ankle.

He dug his nails into my skin, wrenching a cry of pain from my throat. Unable to get him off, I twisted at the waist and drove the knife down into the crux of his shoulder. With an agonized bellow he jerked away from me. I stumbled forward and was caught by Grace. Her arm around my waist kept me upright. I had just enough time to take a full breath before Cooper was on his feet.

"Why are you doing this?"

"I don't have a choice," he seethed, holding the handle of the knife still protruding from his shoulder. He made no attempt to pull it out.

It was difficult to see his expression clearly, but the sound of erratic breathing alluded to rage and pain. He'd clearly lost his mind within the last ten minutes. I didn't want to fight this asshole barefoot in the middle of the woods while some masked lunatic crept up on us.

I looked around trying to figure out how we could get around him without having to go back up the embankment. Movement coming from my left had me whirling in that direction. I swallowed at the sight of yet another masked figure.

This was some real-life horror-fest bullshit, and I was fucking over it. They didn't move, remaining a few feet away. It was hard to make them out entirely, but their build was large, and they looked to be much taller than us.

I didn't know how long they'd been watching or why they were, but I wasn't going to stand here and find out.

When Cooper noticed them, his rage became a tangible fear. The masked figure came down the embankment with measured steps. I moved backward, bumping into Grace.

He paid us no attention, his focus solely on Cooper. As he approached him, Cooper began to blubber an apology, much like Elizabeth had. I couldn't claim to fully understand why either of them had done this, but my gut was telling me they may have known what would happen tonight.

"I did everything he said," Cooper pled.

The man circled him like an animal would prey it was preparing to attack. His movements weren't fast or hurried, but purposely slow. He stopped after his third rotation and reached for the knife still wedged in Cooper's shoulder. He didn't simply pull it out, he twisted the handle and pushed the blade deeper before jerking the knife free in an upward arc.

Cooper's anguished scream echoed across through the woods. He grabbed at his wound and wailed. When the coppery stench of blood reached where Grace and I stood I decided now was the best time for us to make a run for it. With a small push to get her moving, we gave Cooper and the man a wide berth, heading back in the opposite direction.

The continuous pleas for mercy were the only reason we slowed to look behind us. We didn't need perfect vision to understand what happened next. The masked figure grabbed Cooper by the hair and forced his head back, slicing into his throat.

His obscured gaze lifted to where we stood rooted in place just a few feet away. Apparently deciding we weren't worth the effort to pursue, he crouched down and resumed cutting into Cooper's flesh.

CHAPTER FIVE

Once we'd put a decent bit of space between us and what had just happened, we crept back up another embankment. At the top, we both took a moment to catch our breath. I planted my hands on my knees and surveyed the overgrown pathway, my chest rising and falling rapidly.

"What the *hell* was that?"

Grace shook her head slowly. "I-I don't know. One second, he was team us, and the next he was team them. How could he just flip like that? He went from scared to homicidal in the span of seconds."

I didn't have an answer, but she wasn't really expecting one. Rapidly approaching footsteps had a groan of disbelief escaping through my parted lips.

"It's me," Mel announced moments before coming into view. She sounded just as out of breath as we did, but hearing her voice had relief as I'd never known washing over me. As she got closer, I was able to see her top was saturated.

"None of that's yours, right?"

She looked down as if she was just now realizing she'd been covered in a decent amount of blood. "No. This belongs to one of those masked fuckers that tried to drag me deeper into the woods."

Her delivery was so nonchalant I couldn't determine if she'd killed this person or inflicted enough damage that they were lying somewhere wishing she had.

"What happened to you?"

I thought she meant my arm but she reached for my hand, and I realized there was blood on that part of me too.

"It's not all mine."

She visibly relaxed. "You can fill me in later, we're getting our asses outta here."

"Are you the only one that's left besides us?"

"Max is gone, that clown reeled him like a fish. Dion, that fucking redhead, and Hayven already took off. I wasn't leaving without you two."

"How did you know where we were?" Grace asked.

"I didn't. I knew you guys ran the other way and was hoping like I've never hoped before you figured out the paths were traps from the very beginning."

"Lana did," Grace divulged.

Mel glanced back at me. "You were right about which way to go too. Life? Yeah. That was a shitshow."

"And where exactly are these people now?" I asked as we reached the scarecrow we'd separated at.

"That is an excellent question. Let's haul ass so we don't find out."

We navigated our way back through the cornstalks, an eerie type of silence settling in the air now that everyone else had seemingly vanished. The barn had been closed up. No music played and Elizabeth's body was nowhere to be found. There weren't any traces of blood either. It was like the past twenty minutes didn't happen.

We weaved through the next part of the maze, each of us keeping our eyes and ears open. My mind raced ahead, wondering what would happen once we passed through that final gate. I couldn't imagine us being able to simply walk away from all of this. People were just sliced up and murdered for fucks sake.

Mel slowed and looked over at us, her expression somber. "If things start to go bad, I want you two to try and get away. I'll cover you."

"Um, excuse the fuck out of you. This isn't COD, Mel. I'm not going to let you *cover* us."

"Are we supposed to say screw you and run off hoping you fare for the best?" Grace seconded with angry sarcasm. "There are actual murderers somewhere."

"All we have to do is get through the small stretch of woods between here and Sainte's backyard," I reasoned.

"You make it sound so simple," Mel deadpanned.

I ignored her and mentally walked the path in my head. It wasn't that great of a distance to cover, realistically, but as Grace had pointed out people were trying to kill us.

I wondered if Hayven and the others made it. Surely, we would've heard more screaming if they hadn't or some signs of an ensuing struggle.

We came upon the entrance to the cornfield and passed through the arch. The gate slammed shut, prohibiting us from going back. Straight ahead would be a clean shot if it weren't for the small group of masked men waiting for us off to the right.

I stopped dead in my tracks and reached for Mel's arm, prepared to pull her behind me. She shook me off and positioned herself in front of us as the men began to fan out, blocking any path of escape. The clown was here along with the person that slit Cooper's throat. So, there *had* been another way out. He wouldn't have beaten us here otherwise.

A guy sporting a black mask that glowed neon green was the first to speak. "I will be the first to say I'm somewhat impressed. You three didn't do half bad."

"They were scrappy at best. There's room for some much-needed improvement," someone replied objectively.

When one of the men in a black and white mask stepped forward, we instinctively moved back, earning a few amused chuckles.

"I think they're afraid," another asshole goaded.

A guy with the Devil's cross marking his mask glanced at who had spoken, and then back at us. "Liliana isn't. She said so herself."

Holy shit. I blinked as his voice registered. Grace and Mel turned their heads and looked at me with what I'm sure was confusion.

"You're not afraid of me are you, Puppet?"

"...Ciaran?" I questioned slowly, not quite believing what was right in front of me or what I was hearing.

He laughed lowly and reached around Mel to extend a leather-gloved hand. "Come here. I need to get you checked over."

I frowned at his terminology. I wasn't a dog that needed examined for fleas and ticks and going off with him sounded about as appealing as peeling off my own skin.

Mel shoved his arm away. "Fuck off Hannibal, she isn't going *anywhere* with you."

Someone snickered at her chosen nickname. Ciaran didn't share their sense of humor. His head slowly turned in Mel's direction and when he spoke his voice was cold. "This is my one and only warning to you. Don't get in my way. Not when it comes to her. You won't like the consequences.". His attention then redirected to me along with his hand. "Come here."

"You didn't just threaten her and then ask me to hold your hand. Hard fucking pass."

"Also locked us in a barn and then went on a killing spree. No one with a brain would go with you," Grace ranted.

With a heavy sigh, Ciaran swiftly moved my friends out of the way, much too easily, and grabbed me, hoisting my body up and over his shoulder as if I weighed nothing.

Mel and Grace tried to intervene but were quickly thwarted by his buddies. Expletives filled the air as he carried me away from them.

"They won't hurt them," Ciaran assured.

"Like they didn't hurt those other people? Put me *down!*" I twisted my body left and right, slamming a fist into his back.

"Enough." He clapped me on the ass with the palm of his hand and then proceeded to rub away the sting.

"Did you just—?"

"You like that?"

His playful tone pissed me off. Everything about what was happening pissed me off because I didn't understand what was going on.

"Fuck you," I growled.

He laughed softly and continued to carry me until we got to the entrance of the woods.

I was lowered down with a surprising degree of gentleness, all things considered.

"Walk with me or back into my arms you go."

"I'll walk," I bit out.

He grabbed my hand and led me through the backyard. No one paid us any attention aside from a few lewd shouts. Small mercies did exist, I suppose. Unfortunately, they didn't last long.

As we were making our way back into the house, I began to come down from my adrenaline rush, making me acutely aware of the aches and pains on various parts of my body and the cut on my arm.

I had just witnessed, the severing of a hand, a girl's face split in half with an ax and condemned an old classmate to death because he'd tried to plant a knife in me and Grace.

How long ago did I tell myself this night had taken a bizarre turn?

People moved out of Ciaran's way without him saying a word. They might not have immediately recognized me, but he was another story. Why was I letting this homicidal boy take me away?

I didn't know.

Maybe I wasn't really here. I was witnessing it all through an out-of-body experience. That wouldn't be such a far-fetched conclusion after all the shit I'd just seen go down.

"Where are you taking me?" I asked once we reached the staircase.

"I already told you."

Being alone with him would not be smart. If he decided that he wanted to stab something at least down here I could throw one of these random strangers into his blade.

Did he have a knife? I checked his person and couldn't see one. I hadn't earlier either but that didn't mean anything.

Cooper had concealed his.

We returned to the second level and entered a bedroom done in an island theme that had previously been locked and deemed off-limits to party guests. Apparently, that didn't apply to him. A small bedside lamp lit the decent-sized space.

Ciaran led me passed the bed and into an attached bathroom, kicking the door shut behind us. The room remained dark and silent for all of three seconds. He flipped a switch and light spilled from rows of recessed bulbs. He finally let go of my hand and turned to face me, reaching for my mask.

"Let me see you."

My partial disguise was lifted away and set down on one side of the double vanity. Ciaran's joined it before he began an intrusive probe of my entire body.

He took hold of me and placed my ass between the two sinks, positioning himself in-between my legs. I stared at him in wonder.

"So, you just come to parties, kill a few people, and then make sure the survivors have a clean bill of health?"

"Few things wrong with that assessment. I didn't kill anyone tonight and survivors is plural. I'm only standing between your legs right now."

The absolute gall of him. "You know what I meant. Don't treat me like I'm an idiot."

He paused in his probing and momentarily gave me his full attention. "I would never treat you like that. I know you're not stupid, but you are confused and pissed off because you don't know what just happened."

He lifted my hand and examined where my acrylic had torn off and the cracked nail beside it.

My natural nail had broken away with it, leaving the bed beneath raw and bloodied. I was doing my best to ignore the way it throbbed. "I don't know why I'm in here with you right now."

"Yes, you do," he replied confidently, taking another look at the cut on my arm. "It's not deep enough to need stitches."

"I don't think you're the right person to be helping me make sense of what just happened when I'm ninety percent sure you helped make it happen."

"I'm one of the only people that wants you to know what's going on, Lana. The fact you're so clueless tells me those who should have already told you, haven't."

My mind swirled with different ideas of what he could be talking about. *Who* he could be talking about.

"You want me to understand, but you just confused me even more."

"You're not afraid of me."

I blinked at him, my brow furrowing. "We've already established that but seeing as you're going around murdering people for fun I probably should be." I sighed and begrudgingly amended my statement. "Overseeing the murders of people, I mean."

He leaned down, placing his face closer than I was comfortable allowing so that he could examine my legs and feet. I focused on how his fingertips felt traveling across my skin. They lessened the pain by partially distracting me. The cologne he was wearing had an equally soothing effect.

Ciaran being a source of comfort? It was definitely snowing in hell right now.

"You aren't afraid of me because we're not much different and something inside you knows that's true. You've always known."

My brows rose and I couldn't hold withhold an incredulous laugh. Was he likening me to his ability to not bat an eye when people died? If that was what he meant then, of course, we were similar. That could be said for the dozens of others that for any signs of cameras or recording devices.

"Lana," he called my name softly.

I ignored him and turned towards the mirror, pausing when I got my first real look at myself. *Holy shit.* I looked, and this is no exaggeration, like I'd gotten into a fight with a goddamn bear—and lost. Pieces of leaves were stuck in my hair. There were smudges of dirt on my skin along with a few scratches and the thin gash on my arm was surrounded by dried blood.

"I look like complete shit."

"You've never looked more beautiful. You finally lost the shell you're always hiding in."

My eyes shifted to his in the mirror. Sincerity burned in his gaze along with something else I didn't want to acknowledge but couldn't ignore. It had a foreign sensation taking root in my chest as a pesky flutter traveled through my stomach.

"I don't hide," I lied out of habit.

"You do," he retorted matter-of-factly. "I'd say it's a shame you keep such an incredible part of yourself hidden from the people that would understand you the most, but now I know why."

"You know nothing about me." I twisted back around and began trying to ease myself off the vanity. "I have no idea what you're talking about or what is going on, but I need to go. If you go to jail because you got caught doing whatever it is you do here, try not to implicate me."

His entire demeanor changed. He moved closer and caged my body in by bracing his arms on either side of my waist, wedging himself further between my legs. I ignored how good he felt pressed against me and brought a hand to his chest, applying pressure to keep him from coming any closer.

"Do you how many times that's happened? Why would I go to jail for something we've always gotten away with?"

My mouth opened to tell him to back the fuck up until he spoke again.

"That was Judicium."

"What?"

"In that barn. It's something you're pitifully clueless about."

Was that an insult? It didn't really sound like one, but he kept alluding to the fact I was in the dark about whatever this was. He came closer despite my attempt to prevent him from doing so.

Our proximity had my heart beginning to hammer away in my chest.

"Ciaran we--."

He rendered me into silence by brushing his lips against mine. "You weren't supposed to be here tonight."

I stared into his hypnotic blue eyes, searching for answers, disappointed to see they gave nothing away.

"I wasn't," I agreed quietly. "But how did *you* know that?"

"Because your sister wanted me to," he replied simply.

That stopped me short. Lamia was in on this? Oh, hell no. This couldn't be true. Of course, on one hand, her involvement made a lot of damn sense. On the other, I didn't want to believe my beloved sister sent me and my best friends to the escape room from hell.

"It was to protect you," Ciaran continued as if he had a direct link to my thoughts. "All of you."

"*That's* what you call protecting someone? Sending them to play some screwed-up game that can cost them their life?"

"That wasn't the game. If anything, it was the preliminary draft pick."

I stared at him, a million different responses rising to the surface, yet none of them fluent enough for me to vocalize. His eyes slightly narrowed, and he studied me for a few long agonizing seconds, his obscured expression doing nothing good for my nerves.

"I can't keep talking to you about this, not here and not with you being the equivalent of a newborn. It's going to fuck your head up. You'll be no good to me if you're broken."

"I'm nothing to you at all," I refuted.

"We both know that's not true. You're just confused."

"Quit saying that," I snapped, despite him being absolutely right. I had never in all my life been so fucking lost and confused.

I wasn't sure I wanted to know why the Saintes' had a plot of land for massacres behind their house, but it went against who I was to ignore it altogether. I couldn't tell him this, though.

"I think I should just forget this night entirely."

His responding grin was beautifully sinister. "We both know it's far too late for that, Puppet" He stepped away from me, and I hated that I missed his body heat. "Finish getting yourself cleaned up. I'll wait in the bedroom. Everything you need is in the closet over there."

"Wait!" I reached out and grabbed his arm. "Where is my sister, Ciaran?"

"She's not here anymore." He gently removed my hand and left the room, shutting the door behind him.

I was left alone without the luxury of being able to sit and think. I needed to leave this house. I slid off the countertop and went to the closet he'd pointed to. Inside were multiples of the same items, for both guys and girls. It was a little unsettling, to say the least. I hurried to sort through them all, gathering what I would need to make myself look as close to the way I had when I left home.

As I placed everything on the sink and took a hard look at myself in the wideset mirror, what he'd kept calling me settled into my chaotic thoughts.

Puppet?

True to his word, Ciaran was waiting for me in the bedroom. I exited the bathroom feeling somewhat refreshed, but still achy as hell. His eyes lifted from the screen of his cellphone and swept over me from head to toe.

"Not too bad," he remarked.

"It almost sounds like you prefer me bloodied."

"I'd rather see you covered in someone else's blood."

My steps faltered, a faint smile curving my lips. That was sweetly endearing. "Well, I'm sure when you check those news updates of yours, you'll find I've been covered in my own. My parents are going to kill me."

"No, they won't."

I quirked a brow. He sounded rather sure about that, but I knew them far better than he did, obviously. Even cleaned up, this was not the look of someone that went to see a movie. I could already picture their faces as I tried to explain what *did* happen. We already weren't on the best terms.

"Do you happen to have my shoes?"

"On the dresser."

I turned away from him and went to retrieve my heels.

With every step, I silently cursed this whole evening. This was going to hurt like a sonofabitch in the morning.

"You never wondered why you were raised to be so accepting of violence and death?" Ciaran questioned, sounding genuinely curious.

"If you asked me this earlier, I would've said for the same reason you were, but that obviously isn't the case."

I grabbed my heels and cringed at the idea of having to wear them again. My feet felt like I'd walked over hot coals.

Ciaran laughed softly, alerting me he wasn't as far away as he'd been just a few seconds ago. I glanced over my shoulder and blinked in surprise. He was nearly right behind me. I hadn't even heard him move. I slowly turned around, placing myself between him and the dresser.

"Why are you trying to run away from me so fast?"

"I'm not running. I can't waste any more time here, but if I did run could you blame me?"

I looked down as he closed the space between us, watching his shoes align with my polished black toes. Two fingers came to a point just beneath my chin, lifting my gaze back to his. "Don't even think about trying to do something that stupid."

My eyes widened with awe at his brazenness and audacity. I brought my hands to his chest to shove him away from me, scowling when he covered them with his.

"You can relax. Your parents were called away to an emergency meeting. By the time they get home, their precious little demon will be tucked into her own bed."

I ignored his demon goad and wondered how he pulled off maneuvering my parents. I knew Ciaran had far more power than I ever would, which was impressive because not only was he young, but he'd had to of earned every bit of it. We didn't get handed our privilege because mommy and daddy were loaded, not in the way most imagined.

Him having enough sway over someone that my parents could be lured away from home made him even more formidable. Maybe it was better not to know too much more.

"I'm not even going to ask. Whatever you did or plan on doing, it won't fool the security system on my house. It logs every time someone goes in and out. Thanks, though. I think?"

"That's handled too."

I managed to keep my expression impassive when all I really wanted to was gawk at him. My parents were never one for showing emotion beyond the privacy of our home. They always said that would be like flashing a winning hand.

I'd been taught to follow after them and had a pretty impressive poker face under most circumstances.

This was not most circumstances.

"Anything else?" I half-joked.

He smirked. "Your phones are in your middle console along with the fob to the car. There are extra movie tickets too in case you misplaced yours."

I hadn't even realized I'd lost my phone. As for the tickets, those were the least of my concerns. "How did you get my fob?"

His smirk lifted into a grin. "My swine brought it to me."

My mind flashed back to the man in the pig costume that had bumped into me. For someone that prided themselves on being aware of their surroundings, it was utterly embarrassing not to have known I'd been pickpocketed.

"I was wondering why someone decided to celebrate Halloween a few months early."

"It's their chosen method to keep their identity a secret," he explained dismissively. "Your friends are safe and being tended to. Anything else?" he threw my words back at me when I didn't respond.

There was a ton of anything else. I had questions upon questions, but for the sake of my sanity, I shook my head no. I needed time to clearly process what had happened and what he'd already divulged. Then I could begin trying to figure out why I didn't know about any of this.

After regarding me for a few silent seconds, he stepped away and gestured to the door. I made the short trek across the room, carrying my heels, slowing when he reached for me again. I let him hold onto my other hand, ignoring his warmth as much as I could, following him out into the hall.

The party was still going strong, maybe even stronger than it had been before we entered the bedroom together.

I wondered who here knew what happened on the side of the woods and how many were none the wiser, outsiders aside. I stared at the back of Ciaran's head as we made our way toward the stairs. He had such a good handle on what was happening. It brought more questions to mind.

"Why are you helping me?"

"Because it's beneficial for both of us."

"I don't see how. You said I wasn't supposed to be here, but everything that happened says otherwise."

He stopped without warning and let go of my hand. Right there in the middle of the staircase, he turned and slipped his arms around my waist. His hands gripped my hips like a lover would.

"I knew the second you walked through Sainte's front door. It wasn't hard to swap a few names out with you and your friends. There were always going to be eight people in that barn tonight. It just so happened you got to be one of them."

"I could have died." As the words left my mouth, it was the first time this dawned on me. The thought of dying hadn't once crossed my mind. I'd been wholly focused on surviving.

"You're standing here in my arms, alive."

The simplicity of his reply and the way he delivered it pissed me off all over again. I pushed against him, hoping he'd let me go and fall down the damn stairs.

He held me tighter. "You have a lot of reasons to be upset, but this wasn't done to hurt you. I promise."

"That's exactly what it did," I retorted, immediately wishing I hadn't. It was an omission that revealed vulnerability, something he hadn't earned the right to see from me.

He studied my face before leaning closer, placing his mouth beside my ear, he began speaking softly.

"Beneath the spare tire in your trunk is a burner phone. Text me when you're ready to talk."

I slightly leaned away, turning my head so that I could look into his eyes. "What makes you so sure I'll keep my mouth shut or even want to speak to you again?"

He released my hips and brought his hands to my face. Fingers tangled in my hair as he pulled my mouth to his and kissed me. It wasn't soft or gentle. It was bold and borderline possessive. He didn't seek my consent or shyly wait for my submission, he demanded both.

His tongue swept between my parted lips and entwined with mine. As if possessed, I kissed him back, not submitting but giving in to what he wanted. I gripped the hem of his shirt, warming with need like I never had before. Maybe it was the way his hands held me or how his body felt pressed against mine.

I wrapped my arms around his neck and pulled him closer, swallowing back a moan when one of his hands dropped to my ass. I wasn't sure who broke away first. When we finally parted, he stared at my lips, his confliction evident.

Both his hands slowly returned to my waist as he leaned down and whispered victoriously. "That's how I know you'll call me, Puppet."

I swallowed as our gazes collided. The look in his eyes was intensely covetous, threatening to drown me in their brilliant blue depths. I rolled my lips together and breathed him in.

"There were a lot of other ways for you to prove your point."

"I was proving something to both of us. Do you know how long we've waited for this?"

I went completely still, my brain zeroing in on his confession. No matter what kind of fantasies I'd had involving him, I never expected a single one of them to become a reality. I didn't trust him enough to respond honestly, choosing to plead the fifth.

"*This* shouldn't be happening."

"*This* was inevitable," he swore with a touch of anger.

I forced myself to look away, suddenly remembering where we were. Sure enough, we'd garnered a fair amount of attention, which was to be expected. I didn't let anyone put their hands on me. Not even my ex could get away with kissing me like this. Allowing Ciaran to do so was downright scandalous.

"Do you know how many people are watching us right now?"

"Of course, I do." Clasping my jaw, he gently turned my face back towards him. "That's exactly why I did it."

He showed no signs of remorse or regret. Without having to say a word he'd unapologetically told everyone here that I was his.

CHAPTER SIX

You're not supposed to let where you come from define you or shape your future, but it's where I came from that made me who I was and paved the path I was expected to walk. It was the expectancy that made me so determined to be my own person.

A few weeks ago, I graduated early at the top of my class. I suppose that's something I should've been happy about. I'd worked my ass off to achieve honors, but it wasn't done for any kind of self-gratification or for my future.

A diploma meant nothing when you had a golden ticket that guaranteed you'd be riding shotgun straight to hell.

I'd been trying my best not to think about this, but wasn't that how life was supposed to go?

After high school, you planned out your next chapter. Really ambitious people set life goals even before then. I knew some girls that had their weddings planned by the time they were sixteen. My point is, that you made a series of decisions that would shape the rest of your life. I often dreamed of a life where I was that fortunate. Those kinds of decisions weren't in the cards for me.

Not yet anyways.

I could picture the abhorrent looks on my parents' faces if I dared to openly go against their regime. My rebellion was never bold and spontaneous. I weighed the pros and cons, always. Until recently that is. There was nothing like a little murder and the feel of a forbidden kiss to get you twisted up in a mess of secrets.

It'd been two weeks since Sainte's party and with each passing day, my list of questions grew along with the acceptance of what Ciaran had divulged.

I lived in hoodies when I was at home because my family liked to keep the air on frigid, so hiding the marks hadn't been too difficult. My broken nail was explained away without issue. Nails broke sometimes, we got them fixed. Me pretending nothing out of the ordinary happened was the real testament to my acting abilities.

I didn't think I would be able to pull it off. Those first seven days I made sure I didn't slip up, not daring to breathe too hard in case my mother somehow linked that one heavy exhalation to the chaotic night I'd had. The next seven days were spent remembering a certain someone pressed against me and struggling to conceal the tumultuous emotions I'd begun to feel.

More concerning was that I hadn't heard a word from my sister since that night. Her phone went straight to voicemail for two days before ultimately being disconnected.

I'd tapped all the resources I had to see if there'd been any sightings of her, but thus far there hadn't been a single one. It was as if she'd vanished. Unfortunately, my only other option was guaranteed to have a catch.

For Lamia, it would be worth it, but I had to consider my own well-being when it came down to attempting to make a deal with him. That's *if* he would help me. I didn't have much I could offer in return.

I wasn't the only one frustrated with past and current events. Mel rolled onto her stomach and stared at me from the opposite side of the massive L-shaped sectional. I saw her in my peripheral and tried to ignore the look she was giving me. Grace served as a barrier between us with her legs propped up on the ottoman.

"You should make the call."

I pretended to pull my attention away from the cinema screen none of us were really watching. "What call?"

"Lana." Her tone said it all.

"I just don't trust him—*them*."

"You're not even a little interested in hearing what *he* has to say about your sister or what Judicium was?"

I gave her a mock glare. Of course, she caught my slip-up and *of course*, she was hitting on the money. Mel had witnessed the whole staircase spectacle and only let it go four days ago. Now she'd moved on to this.

I'd been fighting with myself daily not to use the burner phone still hidden away in the well of my spare tire. I initially only sought it out so that I could make sure it wasn't turned on. It would be hard to explain why my trunk was ringing if someone else at the house heard it go off.

Ever since I'd seen the phone with my own two eyes, I thought of it and the kiss that shouldn't have happened entirely way too much, among other things.

"I don't think they'll hurt us," Grace claimed in a quiet voice.

Mel and I shared a look before settling our gazes onto our pretty blonde friend. Her eyes darted between the two of us. When she shifted uncomfortably, I bit back a smile. We knew each other too well.

"Ky seems nice, that's all."

"You mean *Michael Myers* reincarnation?" Mel deadpanned.

"Don't call him that. I'm being serious."

I worried my lip, wondering just how much she'd spoken to this guy. I *knew* of him, but I didn't *know* anything concrete beyond basic information you could find anywhere. For example, he was the polar opposite of her. He was the epitome of an apex predator. She would be his prey. His twin wasn't much better, but at least he could be around people without putting them into a state of terror.

After being filled in about what happened during our brief time apart, I'd come to learn which mask Kyrous had been wearing.

"This is the one that slit Cooper's throat, right?" *And hacked off his head.*

Her features softened and she nodded. "Yeah. Like I said, I don't think they'll hurt us."

I wasn't understanding how that canceled out him being dangerous. I could tell Mel was thinking the same and seconds away from opening her mouth to stick her foot in it. I shot her a look that said to do otherwise. If Grace thought he was harmless, she had to have her reasons. She had me and

Mel to stop her from doing anything too hazardous.

"When did you last talk to him?" I asked, genuinely curious.

"I wouldn't really say we talk. He texts me sometimes."

"Oh, really. What's he send you? Pictures of dismembered bodies?" Mel joked dryly.

I rolled onto my side as a sudden thought occurred to me. "You gave him your number?"

"No, of course not! The number he texts me from was already saved in my phone."

"Are you sure it's a good idea to communicate with him at all?"

Grace frowned. "Well, it can't be traced back to him. It's one of those texting apps or something. I looked it up."

She missed my point entirely. Bless her naïve heart. I hoped she never got so tainted by our world that it was snatched away. It was one of my sole missions to keep it safe.

"How does that make him trustworthy?" Mel continued to prod.

"That's not what I'm saying. If they wanted to hurt us, they could have. It isn't like the opportunity didn't present itself multiple times."

I sighed and sat up, running a hand through my hair. "She has a point."

"If she has a point then so do I," Mel retorted.

"Now you're contradicting yourself. And I wasn't finished. Yeah, she makes a good point, but they did lock our asses inside of a barn and make us do the Hokey-Pokey with our lives."

Hearing the entry chime of an exterior door opening followed by a set of heels clicking across the marble floor, I held a finger to my lips. A minute or so later my mother appeared in the doorway of the cinema room.

"Hey," I greeted her with a smile I hoped came off as genuine.

It must have because she returned it with one of her own.

"I knew I heard something in here. Have you been home all day?"

This was a question that didn't need an actual answer. My family kept tabs on me religiously. It was a miracle she hadn't found out about Sainte's party. I still wasn't entirely sure she hadn't figured out I'd been there. Pandora Serpine didn't give anything away unless she wanted to. My mother was nothing but confident, level-headed, and ruthless.

If she wasn't my mom, she'd be one of the rare few I found to be terrifying. My whole life I'd been told that I was just like her. While I couldn't deny looking at her sometimes felt like looking in a mirror, our resemblance is where any similarities came to an end.

Our personalities couldn't be more different.

I was more like my late *Abuela*. This had never been a point of contention between us until I hit my senior year. My parents trying to force my path put a damper on our relationship.

They wanted me to go one way and I was convinced I was going to go another. This bullshit with Lamia provided me a solid argument to back my budding resentment. I could never forgive them for how they treated her. I was slightly comforted by the fact that my *Abuelo* had gone on a trip shortly after and was yet to return. Even my older brother had put noticeable distance between them since that incident and he was the golden child.

I couldn't be too ecstatic over their disagreement when Ciaran's words implied my entire family was keeping something from me that I was entitled to know. Mel and

Graces too, which wasn't surprising considering their parents were best friends with mine.

He hadn't said it was them directly, but they were the only ones that fit his roundabout accusation.

Nobody else owed me any kind of explanation. It made more sense every time I thought about it.

We'd found out which families those who perished at Sainte's party belonged to, but nothing came of their disappearances.

All their social media accounts vanished less than forty-eight hours later. It was as if they'd been erased entirely from existence. That wasn't something you could do with a few clicks of a button. Not unless you were doing it from a position of power.

Looking at my mother at that moment, I made up my mind about the phone. I couldn't outright ask her about this or if she'd done something to my sister. Lamia's name had become taboo in our house.

She'd been erased in the same way that Cooper, Elizabeth, and Max had.

It was infuriating. I burned with bitterness and guilt for not doing more to find her.

Logically, I could never go against my family and win. That didn't take away the shame of being so powerless. At this point, I was desperate, and sometimes desperation called for dangerous measures.

"We were just about to head out for some *Charley's.*"

"I need those loaded fries in my life," Mel added with convincing enthusiasm.

"Oh, that does sound good."

Mom reached up and began to remove the pins holding her long dark hair in an immaculate chignon. "Can you bring me something back? *Papá* has a late-night, so I was going to order in for us, anyways."

"You could always come with," I suggested, already knowing she wouldn't.

"I still have some things to take care of. Rain check, okay? You girls go head and enjoy yourselves. I'll be working until he's home."

"Okay, just text what you want."

She thanked me and left us alone, the sound of her eight-inch heels fading as she headed towards the staircase.

She'd work out, take a shower, and then lock herself away in her office. Same routine as always when her schedule had nothing else on it.

"So, *Charley's*?" Grace prompted.

"Good food and a chance to get out of the house. That's a win-win." I hit pause on our movie and tossed my throw aside.

Nibbling on a fry, I stared at the phone in my hand.

It was a brand I had never seen before, close to prehistoric. You had to tap a button multiple times for each letter. I wondered where Ciaran got it from. Even my *Abuelo* had an Apple.

"It's been twenty minutes," Mel pointed out, sipping her strawberry shake.

"Maybe he's busy."

Grace leaned between the cream-colored seats with a knowing smile. "Do you want me to call?"

"No," I grumbled, going to the only contact saved in the phone.

I hit the green button and managed to find the speaker phone just as it connected.

"I was wondering how long it would take for you to call," Ciaran stated as soon as he answered, placing heavy emphasis on the word *call*.

"I'll give you ten minutes to explain what it is you want me to know."

"Five," Mel corrected.

Someone laughed in the background on Ciaran's end.

"I won't need that."

"I'm waiting."

"There's somewhere I need you to go first."

I glanced at Grace and Mel to make sure they'd heard the same thing I just did. "Go? I don't think I need to tell you this, but our parents keep us under a microscope."

"They aren't the only ones."

"Huh?"

"Do you know of a place where tragedy and drama meet every night?"

My brows furrowed as I considered the question. There was only one place that immediately came to mind. "I think so…"

"On Friday you're going to be there by six."

"Are you being serious?"

"Six on the dot. Don't be late and get rid of the phone."

That wouldn't be a problem. He had me ready to launch it out the window.

I kept my composure and maintained level-headedness. "Why can't you just talk to me now?"

"It's better this way. Trust me."

"I don't."

"If you want something from me, you should start. Your sister did."

There he went bringing up Lamia again. His casual way of talking about her, as if they were well acquainted, planted an unpleasant seed in my mind.

"Place this phone in the rest of your lemonade and pitch it before going home."

My eyes immediately dropped to the cup holder where my half-empty drink sat. "How did you know I had a lemonade?"

The call ended without him answering me. I stared at the screen until it went black and then looked at Grace and Mel.

How did he know where we were?

CHAPTER SEVEN

On a prominent stretch of city real estate, you could find the Eden Theater. It was a restored movie and showtime venue with an attached hotel that screamed of money the moment you stepped into the lobby.

After little deliberation, it was decided by the three of us that this was the only place that fit Ciaran's purposely vague description. It also happened to be one of the few spots we chose to frequent when needing a reason to get away for a night.

Something told me he was aware of this too but that didn't bother me for the reasons one might think. I whipped my Range Rover into the parking lot with five minutes left till six.

Having no idea what kind of car Ciaran would be in, I reversed into an empty space between a large black pickup and a small sedan.

"Any sign of him?"

"Not yet," Grace replied, stretching up off the backseat to see over the cars on either side of us.

Mel and I surveyed what we could of the parking lot. The place wasn't exactly empty, and the sun had begun to set. Without the burner phone, there wasn't a way to contact him. I didn't like that, but I understood why I needed to get rid of it.

"You bought our tickets already, right?" I double-checked with Mel.

"Three for *Notre Dame De Paris*. Grace's favorite. They've already been hole-punched and are safely in the glovebox."

"Okay, good." I checked the time and then surveyed the parking lot again.

At six on the dot, a silver SUV came to a stop directly in front of my parking spot. The windows were tinted to an illegal degree, making it impossible for us to see who was driving.

"That has to be him," Mel said quietly.

"Guess we're about to find out."

When the driver of the SUV stepped into my line of vision it wasn't Ciaran, but one of his friends, Maverick Stolas. He peered through the windshield and offered a friendly wave. I took that as a sign we were supposed to go and talk to him. It didn't escape my notice that he was by himself.

"You guys ready?"

Mel twisted her lips and looked over at me. "Is that rhetorical?"

With a roll of my eyes, I placed my fob in the clutch I'd chosen to match my dress and reached for the door handle.

I slipped out of the car and waited for them to do the same so that we'd be together.

"Don't you all look beautiful," Maverick proclaimed before casually demanding we give him our phones.

Grace eyed him warily. "Why?"

He grinned and slipped his hands into the pocket of his black hoodie. "Safety precautions."

"And where is Ciaran?" Mel questioned suspicion bleeding into her tone.

"Waiting. We can go to him as soon as you relinquish the phones. You'll get them back when we're done."

I hesitated for another second before begrudgingly popping open my clutch to remove my cell and hand it over. I knew this wouldn't be a simple endeavor.

"Why thank you," he lilted, tucking it right into his hoodie pocket before accepting Grace's.

"Maybe this wasn't such a great idea," Mel muttered once she'd handed him hers.

Maverick stepped back and openly checked her out. "I think it was a fantastic idea. Is that navy? It's *definitely* your color."

His enthusiasm had me suppressing a smile. She did look good. There weren't too many times she didn't. Wearing a dress went against my better judgement considering the barn incident, but we had to adhere to Eden's guidelines.

Grace and I had opted for black pieces that were more or less the same style as Mel's—short, tight, and not at all appropriate for this meeting. I didn't have a variety of other options to choose from. I couldn't exactly where one of the gala gowns or cocktails was when I always dressed like this for these events. I didn't want to garner my parents' attention by suddenly switching it up.

Mel wasn't a fan of the flattery and her expression conveyed that.

"Can we go wherever it is we're going?"

"Come on." His smile never slipped, he lifted his chin and indicated for us to get in the truck after taking another look at her.

Maverick wasn't too bad on the eyes either, even in nothing but denim and a hoodie. His dark hair and nearly black eyes sharpened his jagged edges. He had a gorgeous smile and the kind of bad-boy charm that got good girls in trouble. Thankfully we didn't fit such criteria.

We settled ourselves in the car, me up front, Mel and Grace in the back. Maverick opened the middle console and removed a slim metal pick resting at the bottom. Without a word, he took each of our cellphone cases off and then used the tool to pop open our sim card trays and remove them.

"What are you doing?"

"Being cautious in case your parents track your phones."

I never knew if they did that for sure, but it had been a long-standing suspicion so for him to suspect the same thing practically confirmed it.

"Is that really the reason?" Mel asked.

"I'm doing this right in front of you, so you know where they are," he remarked, placing all three phones into the center compartment along with their sim cards once they were powered down.

"But you have to turn your phones off in the theater. They can't track them that way," Grace pointed out.

Maverick shifted the truck into drive with a nod of his head. "Exactly. There's a small probability they could turn back on. That's one risk no matter how slight we're not going to take."

I couldn't find a reason to argue with him, but the level of caution regarding this meet-up was proving to be more thorough.

Maverick pulled out of the parking lot and slid me a glance. "Are you more of a country or R&B, girl?"

When I didn't reply, he reached for his stereo and began tapping away at the screen with a murmured, "Jazz it is."

I sighed and propped my hand on my chin, looking out the window for some sign of where we were going.

I recognized the building right away. It belonged to a family mine wanted nothing to do with for reasons that were beyond my time.

If our parents were, in fact, tracking us I would be forever grateful someone deemed it necessary for our phones to be disabled. If they knew we were here they'd lose their minds.

"Privacy," Maverick said as a way of explanation for our destination.

He pulled into the lower parking deck and parked close to a set of doors that led inside. There wasn't much conversation as we exited the SUV and entered the building with a specialized keycard. Once we went down a short hall, a private lift took us the rest of the way to our meeting spot, a luxury penthouse.

If I'd known this was where we'd be going, I wouldn't have come. Being alone with these guys was already testing my nerves. Being alone with them thousands of feet above the ground with only one known exit seemed suicidal. I had come this far now, though.

I wasn't going back without some kind of viable explanation or help to find my sister.

"Ladies first," Maverick smoothly insisted.

"You don't want to check my bag or pat me down?"

"I would, but I value my limbs." He noted my confusion with a boyish grin. "He promised to cut off my hands if I touched your strings."

Still not sure what he was talking about, I took a quick breath to calm my nerves and stepped off the lift. My lacey flat went from shined marble to flushed concrete. The temperature dropped significantly due to the AC.

Maverick sidled passed me and motioned for us to follow him down a hall lined with rich-colored trim. There was a freshness in the air along with a hint of pine.

Everything looked immaculately clean, not at all the bachelor's pad I'd been envisioning. I wondered if all of them lived together.

I glanced over my shoulder at Mel and Grace to see if they were okay, getting a smile and thumbs up.

Voices grew louder in volume, remaining soft in tone until we entered a living room filled with plush ivory furniture. A massive floor-to-ceiling window made up the back wall, giving a beautiful view of the city lit up beneath us.

Ciaran stood from where he'd been sitting the second he saw me. He was dressed down in jeans and a simple t-shirt and still looked as good as he did when I saw him in suits and tuxedos.

Struck by the full weight of his intensive stare I came to a stop in front of a large television that had been mounted on an accent wall above a fireplace.

Grace and Mel stood beside me, their eyes taking in the room.

"You can sit down," he prompted.

"Yeah, it's not like we're deranged killers or anything," Charon quipped with thinly veiled amusement.

I began to object but then thought better of it. I didn't want to stand in the center of the room like an item on display. I walked over to two plush-looking armchairs and perched on the arm of one, leaving the actual cushions for Mel and Grace.

Ciaran sat down on the end of the larger sofa, close to me, placing Charon to his immediate left. His brother remained in the same spot he had been, a loveseat that was aligned with Grace's chair on the opposite side of the room.

I rested my clutch across my thighs to add more coverage, crossing my legs at the ankle.

Wanting to get straight to it, I made a point not to look at Ciaran directly and focused on the room as a whole.

"Why are we here?"

"To talk."

"About?" Mel challenged.

Ciaran leaned back and looked at Maverick. He cleared his throat and stepped forward.

"We wanted to explain what happened at the party."

"The game...?"

"That was Judicium," Kyrous corrected me.

I think this was the first time I'd ever heard him speak. It wasn't my first time hearing that word, though, thanks to Ciaran. I belatedly recalled it's what had been carved into the top of the archway leading into the corn maze.

"Judicium means judgement. It's what the land the barn sits on is for until the next location is constructed," Charon explained.

"But what's being judged? All we did was try to solve some riddle that got a guy's hand cut off and then run through the woods." Mel pushed for clarification.

Maverick crossed his arms and leaned against the wall beside the television. "That's what was being judged. Your ability to think, act, and if or when necessary, kill."

Grace clasped her hands together on her lap. "It wasn't random?"

"Most people are willing participants. They know it's expected of them if their families wish to name them as an official heir when the head steps down."

"And the ones that have no idea what this is?" I asked.

"Is usually so rare it's unheard of," Charon answered.

Mel scoffed. "So, everyone else knew what was going to happen that night? Their fear was pretty convincing."

"Most aren't like you three." Maverick smiled at her. "Just because people know they're going to have to do something terrifying doesn't make them fearless."

I didn't appreciate his honesty in this regard. I studied the floor and tried to wrap my head around this. "My sister trusted you with something, what was it?"

"Isn't that obvious? You," Maverick stated.

"She couldn't keep you safe and knew all about the game. She went through Judicium years ago. None of us believed her when she said you didn't know what it was. Turns out she was telling the truth."

I turned and looked at Ciaran directly and finally asked what had been bugging me since the thought came to mind. "Are you the one that got her pregnant?"

Maverick smothered a laugh by pretending to clear his throat again. Ciaran's eyes went glacial. He clearly didn't like the implication. He leaned forward and made sure he had my full attention. "The only Serpine I'd ever waste a single breath on, is you. Never forget that."

He said my family name as if it were riddled with disease. If he didn't like them then Grace and Mel's families were on his shit list too. It was the timeless divide I'd heard about all my life.

He and his friends belonged on one side and us on the other. The Belair's were morally no better than Serpines, though. So where was this hatred coming from and why did Lamia trust them enough to bring me and Ciaran together.

"Okay, now that we've established none of us like one another--."

"I never said I didn't like her," he interrupted Mel.

Maverick snapped his fingers to summon our attention. "Listen, I've got the cliff notes. You three should know all about the game because typically, you'd be the one doing all killing after your inductions. Since you're all so oblivious we assume, and I can bet my asshole, you are going to be highly bid-on contestants from start to finish."

There was an unspoken *if you live that long* hanging at the end of his sentence.

"Can you maybe add some enlightenment? Contestants for a game where we *kill* people or get killed?" I queried, not buying this was an actual thing.

The barn incident I could believe because I'd been there. I knew our families had wealth and shady ass people of power in their pockets. Getting away with murder was done as easily as Maverick had just snapped his fingers, but this was extreme.

"Puppet, if you don't kill them, they'll take immense pleasure in killing you."

"Especially given who your family is," Charon added. "They've already got some master scheme for the new playground."

Maverick bobbed his head in agreement. "I didn't even consider that. The bids that would come in for just one of you being on the wrong side of the game full throttle would be insane. The spectators would love it."

"Spectators?" I repeated in a sad attempt at keeping up with the foreign language he was speaking.

"It's a lot of complicated parts to this. We don't want to overwhelm you," Ciaran said in a way that warned Maverick he needed to stop talking.

"So, our families will just send us off to die?" Grace asked

"No. That is never the goal, especially when it comes to your family. Heirs are the foundation," Ciaran explained. "As I said, there's a lot that goes into it."

Grace sighed and rubbed her temple, "This is unbelievable."

"You better start believing because Judicium was child's play. In our reality you don't get to leave and go home at the end of the day," Kyrous stated with a roll of his shoulders.

Mel laughed dryly. "Are we going to be locked away and forced to play along?"

"Yes," Charon replied matter-of-factly.

I could tell by the energy in the room and their serious expressions that they were being serious. That didn't make it any easier to accept. If Lamia was aware of this, she'd been keeping more from me than I thought.

If she wanted me to get involved with Ciaran, she had to have a reason, a pretty damn good one. The night of Judicium, he said it was to keep me safe. I was beginning to have a hunch on who she wanted me protected from.

Ciaran's next words further solidified the culprits in question.

"We have a theory on why your families have been keeping you in the dark, but right now it's better if you're none the wiser."

I worried my lip and sat back. "You never said why you decided to drag us into this at my sister's behest."

Ciaran gave me a look as if he was the one confused. "You think I'm doing this because of...? Lana, I don't give a fuck about your sister. That had nothing to do with my decision."

"But you know where she is?" I challenged.

"I have a general idea, but it isn't something I would tell you."

"Where is my sister?" I asked again with a calmness that was at odd with the tumultuous emotions warring inside my head and chest.

"I do not like repeating myself, so stop asking the same questions."

I'm not sure what happened exactly in my thought process. One second, I was on the arm of the chair and the next I was damn near straddling his lap with a hand wrapped around his throat. "Where the fuck is my sister?"

No one made a move to get me off him. Grace stood when Charon did. Mel remained seated. There was a glare on her face that I couldn't see aimed at the other two people in the room as if daring them to try her.

"I think this is the first time you've been a bottom, C. How does it feel?" Maverick joked.

Ciaran's eyes traveled from the hem of my dress to mine, a grin slowly spreading across his face. "I think I could get used to it, but you know better than that. I'm always on top."

He slipped his hands beneath my dress and grabbed my ass. Grabbing two handfuls, he hefted me up and flipped our position.

Charon laughed as his brother walked around to our side of the room. Grace positioned herself behind the armchair as if that would stop him from getting to her.

"Should we fight too?" Charon asked Mel playfully.

"Not if you want your balls to remain between your legs."

"Get off me," I snapped at Ciaran.

"Don't be like that. You propositioned me first," he teased with an antagonizing grin. "If I let you go, will you be good, and do as I say?"

"Do I look like a bitch that obediently follows commands?"

"Hmm." He cocked his head to the side as if truly considering the question. "Your parents seem to think so."

His words rubbed an already sore spot, prodding at the anger burning in my gut. I pushed myself up. He shoved me back down onto the couch with enough force to knock the air from my lungs. "You're not quite in control, are you? Someone has to pull those strings of yours."

He grabbed both of my forearms and pinned them on either side of me. I slammed my head back into the cushion when he lurched down, bringing us to eye level. He came closer and murmured softly. "Unless you want your friends to watch you get fucked every way imaginable, save the foreplay for when we're alone."

I silently cursed my debauched desires, clenching my thighs together. This was bullshit. I didn't spend hours taking self-defense classes to wind up pinned down and defenseless. Another rush of anger had me attempting to headbutt him.

He moved back as if he'd been anticipating the move. With another infuriating grin, he slowly shook his head. "We're going to have a lot of fun together."

"There is no *we*, motherfucker."

His dickhead friends laughed, watching the two of us as if we were prime-time television come to life.

"I want to help you," Ciaran amended, his expression morphing to one of somberness. "Here us out. I promise you it will be worth it."

When I made no move to attack him again, he slowly released me and sat down on the coffee table. I calmed myself as much as I could and sat forward eyeing him with suspicion. "What am I really doing here, Ciaran?"

"I want you to know before any of this happened, I'd made my mind up about you."

"I'm not following."

He expelled a heavy sigh and studied me a beat. "I know you came here wanting help to find your sister. Our interests are somewhat similar. I want to help my brother."

My mouth opened and closed but nothing came out. I crossed my arms and stared, waiting for him to continue.

"Since when do you have a brother?" Mel asked without her usual hostility.

"He's considered by societal terms a half-brother. My father had him before he finally committed to my mother. We thought he'd gone missing. He simply volunteered himself to enter a world he doesn't understand thinking he could save your sister."

"Your brother got Lamia pregnant," Grace summarized the obvious, her tone soft and understanding.

Ciaran looked away, staring out the floor-to-ceiling window behind the sofa. "I told him not to get in bed with snakes."

I took that stinging insult on the chin. It wasn't the first time I'd heard it. There were far more concerning matters at hand than my pride. A sickening realization was spreading through my chest.

If my family knew Ciaran's brother was the one Lamia was seeing, it would cause a fallout of epic proportions, and it had. The half-brother issue would be the cherry on top. She'd been disowned and essentially kicked out onto the streets for her dalliance.

After weeks of silence, she'd vanished again right after reaching out to me. There were very few people who would know she'd done that. My parents topped the list. All they had to do was check the usage history on our phone bill and they'd see her incoming texts. My stomach twisted as I weaved more of this together.

They couldn't see the messages themselves, but that would be enough to set them off. It was such a stupid fucking mistake. I looked at Ciaran and refrained from asking if they'd been the ones who put her wherever she was. I knew the answer.

He'd already alluded to them knowing about everything else.

"So, none of you know where she or the brother is?" I checked.

Maverick winced and rubbed the back of his neck. "We're doing our best."

I shook my head and ran a hand over my brow. "What do I have to do to help?"

Ciaran's blue eyes met with mine and something close to a smirk curled one side of his lips. "You're going to make a deal with the devil."

I leaned forward and mirrored his position. "And what am I supposed to bargain with?"

"Uh, Lana." Grace stepped towards us as if to stop me and was promptly halted by Kyrous wrapping an arm around her from behind.

"You too," he monotoned.

"No shit her too. Lana isn't doing anything with you assholes alone," Mel proclaimed.

Charon looked at her openly amused. "That's not what he meant."

"You three are a package deal," Maverick chimed in.

Leaning back, I placed my hands on my lap and studied Ciaran through slightly narrowed eyes. "What does that mean?"

They did that thing again, where they passed some kind of coded message we couldn't understand. Now it was me who regretted asking such a question.

"You asked what the devil wanted. What if I said it was you?"

I tilted my head and looked at him quizzically. *Me?*

"Haven't I been telling you this entire time I want to help you?"

"Yes, but…" It couldn't be that simple. There had to be something he wasn't telling me—us. A lot of things, actually. He'd already divulged more than anyone else ever had, though.

I wasn't foolish enough to believe it was because he'd been madly in love with me this entire time. Whatever he was after, whatever his reasoning, it was important. "How does helping *me*, help *you*?"

He looked at me the same way he had on the staircase, with a twisted sense of possessiveness burning in his eyes. "The enemy of my enemy is my greatest asset, Puppet."

Ah. Now, this was an angle that made sense and I could honestly get on board with.

Alone I couldn't do a damn thing if I were to go against my family, but having someone like him on my side changed everything.

"Then I guess you have a deal," I stated casually, hoping the sound of my pounding heart couldn't be heard by everyone in the room.

Ciaran's smirk faded and he turned to look at Maverick. "Good thing you prepped the knife."

Had I missed something? "Why do we need a knife?"

Grace broke away from Kyrous with a scowl. "There's no way you're being serious. Why would you do that?"

"What is it?" I questioned, looking between them. I wasn't as quick to catch on

"It's a life sentence," she spat angrily at Ciaran's back.

When I finally connected the dots, I pulled in a small intake of breath.

Ciaran rose from the coffee table and offered me his hand. With a grim twist of my mouth, I reached out and accepted it.

CHAPTER EIGHT

The only light came from a dimmed chandelier and a few candles placed strategically around the room. Two vials sat on either side of a round metal bowl. A curved dagger rested on a black cloth in front of them.

We'd moved from the formal living room to the dining area that was overlooked by a modernized kitchen. Standing around a table of tempered glass, I was moments away from sealing a deal I would never be able to renege on.

This was quite possibly the most reckless thing I'd ever decided to do. It was like signing a contract without understanding the fine print.

There were the blood oaths in movies and fiction, and then there were the oaths exclusive to our society. They were done to unify families for generations or form alliances.

It was ironic to me I'd sworn off marriage and relationships only weeks ago and now I was tying myself to someone with an oath that was sacred and lasted beyond death. It wasn't someone that loved me or vice versa, but the one person I was expressly forbidden to get involved with.

I couldn't think of a better fuck you to anyone who would object or deny this oath. Not if they had a hand in hurting my sister or planning to use my friends.

"You know if our families find out about this the apocalypse will reign down on earth," Mel insinuated.

"Not our families, just yours," Ciaran countered.

"You mean they won't gather their armies and ride at dawn?"

He flashed me a grin and reached for the dagger. "Every family has its secrets, but mine isn't quite as fucked up as yours."

I had nothing to retaliate with. I couldn't bring myself to defend them. "You don't have any STDs or anything, right?"

"I'm going to pretend you didn't just ask me that. Give me your hand."

I reached across the table and allowed him to flip my palm upward. Mel and Grace stood on either side of me for moral support.

"What is it you want?"

I masked my expression before my confusion could mar it. I'd never gotten to learn about this in-depth yet. My parents had claimed it was because they wanted me to be older. Now I wondered if it was really because they didn't want me doing something like this.

It would be unacceptable for me to choose the man I wanted to give this kind of promise on my own.

"I want--."

"Don't say your sister," Ciaran interrupted.

"Helping you is a given. That isn't something you ask of your partner. Expressing what you want is different. No one other than you can feel or hear your thoughts," Kyrous surprisingly filled in some of the blanks.

I wasn't ready to admit what I truly wanted out loud. It was silly, but it mattered to me.

"We won't judge," Maverick assured, sensing my inner conflict.

I was saved from replying when Ciaran took the initiative to go first. He gave my hand a gentle squeeze and winked so subtly that I almost missed it.

"Listen closely, try to remember that I'm not a fan of repeating myself." With our gazes locked together, he brought the tip of the dagger to my palm, not yet pressing down. "I only want you, Puppet. I have everything else."

I forced my hand to remain steady as he began to press the blade into my skin. There was a sharp sting and some pressure as it cut into me. He drew a line from my thumb to the edge of my palm.

Charon made sure the blood that dripped landed in the bowl while Maverick uncapped one of the vials and held it up to begin catching whatever he needed. I had no idea why that was necessary but chose to keep my mouth shut.

"You'll be loyal only to me. If anyone ever touches what's mine, I'll be forced to make you watch as I tear them apart," Ciaran made another line.

I bit my tongue and drew in a quiet breath. This one was right beside the first.

"Double lines for two lifetimes," Grace stated, catching me off guard. How did *she* know?

There was only one more to go and I at least understood what this one was from hearing my *Abuelo* mention it about my *abuela*.

A third that tied us together and represented the three outlooks on life. Past, present, and future. They would be implicitly woven with his. As he readied himself for the final cut, that same look he'd had before returned. The hairs on the back of my neck rose and my stomach somersaulted with nerves. It took Mel placing a reassuring hand on my lower back to restrengthen my resolve.

"You're going to give me everything," Ciaran vowed, marking me with a final pull of the blade.

I forced back a hiss, pulling my gaze from his. My blood dripped steadily, pinging into the bowl. Maverick capped the vial while Kyrous took hold of my wrist to keep my arm extended.

Ciaran grabbed the cloth and wiped the blade before flipping it around, offering me a chance to do what he had. "Would you like to add your terms?"

"They're the same as yours," I replied without thought. I realized my mistake when he grinned devilishly. He flipped the knife back around and began marking himself.

"I pledge this blade and blood, as I pledge to you my soul, forever at your service.". He pressed our bloodied palms pressed together and sealed the deal.

I watched our blood mix together and drip into the bowl.

"You can work out the rest," he said to his friends, passing the knife to Charon.

Looking over at me, he walked around the table, still holding my hand over the top of it. Mel was forced to step out of the way as I moved closer to him. Once I was by his side, he paid none of them any attention.

"Where are we going?" I asked as he guided me away from the table and down another hall, this one lined with solid black doors.

"It's the equivalent of our wedding night, Puppet. I'm going to make you mine in every way that I can."

We entered the third door on the right. From the scent alone I would know we were in his bedroom. The notes of his cologne were stronger in here.

I took in the massive California king with a black and red bedding set. The large marble bed had two matching dressers and an ottoman situated around the room. A plush leather recliner was angled towards the bed a few feet away.

There weren't any pictures on the walls, but one of Ciaran with his family sat on a nightstand in front of a lamp giving the space a soft glow. Two additional doors were on either side of the room.

I assumed one was a closet and the other a bathroom. I turned towards him trying not to think of why he'd bring me in here and saw he'd been watching me the whole time. I made a show of looking around the room again.

"I feel like we just did something demonic."

"We did make an oath that pays respects to the one we worship down below."

"How poetic."

He laughed lightly. "You don't need to be nervous. I promise I'll make it good for you."

That did not help. I swung my gaze towards his and my pulse spiked. The ache between my legs grew in response to the way he was looking at me.

I forced myself to focus on something else. I glimpsed down and his solid print caught my attention first, followed by a small puddle of crimson.

"We're getting blood all over the floor."

He wound our fingers together and wordlessly pulled me closer, locking our bloodied hands together behind my back as he brought my body flush against his.

"We're about to get a lot bloodier than this, Puppet."

"Ciaran…" I trailed off, unsure what I was trying to say.

He cupped my jaw with his other hand and tilted my head back, silencing any objections with his lips and tongue. It began somewhat gentle but neither of us wanted soft or tender. He nipped me, eliciting a low whimper, soothing the sting with the tip of his tongue. Dropping his hand to my throat, he collared me and began to move forward, forcing my body to go backward.

He didn't break our kiss until the back of my knees met with his mattress. He pulled our bloodied hands apart and pushed me down onto the bed.

My back sank into silk and plush bedding as soft as a cloud. It smelled of him, heightening my perception of what we were doing. I stared up at him acutely aware that my lips were probably puffy, and my face was flushed. My dress had risen to a beyond decent level, revealing the black G-string I'd worn beneath it.

"You look like you belong here," he murmured, running his bloody palm up my leg. I shuddered as he got closer to my apex, forcing myself to remain still.

Music began to play throughout the apartment, giving us another layer of privacy. I wasn't sure that was a good thing.

My breath hitched as his hand reached where the fabric of my G-string covered me and pulled it aside.

His gaze dipped between my legs seeing my undeniable arousal. I'd never been gladder I kept myself trimmed.

"Your pussy is just as pretty as you, Puppet."

My face heated in response. He stepped back, removing his shirt before making quick work of his jeans. My mouth dried as I drank in the perfection that was his body. I never knew he had so many tattoos.

I took in his abs that I wanted to trace with my tongue, halting on the outline I couldn't miss. Ciaran shoved down his boxers and my stomach flipped with a fluttering sensation. His dick was *huge* and *thick*. A vein ran from the tip to the base surrounded by a patch of dark curls.

"Take your dress off," he commanded softly.

I bit my lip and slowly complied. Sitting up, I bunched the tight material in both hands and lifted it over my head.

I reached back and unhooked my bralette next, leaving me in nothing but the G-string. I was comfortable in my skin and didn't attempt to hide from his hungry stare. His eyes took in every inch of me, feeling like a heated caress.

His low groan of appreciation coupled with the look on his face had me growing hotter. I pressed my legs together in an attempt to alleviate the throbbing sensation.

"You are too fucking beautiful for words."

The compliment brought a smile to my face. He laughed lowly and climbed back onto the bed. Gripping both my knees, he pushed them apart and settled his solid body between my legs. He kissed my lips and my jaw and then began kissing my neck.

I sighed contentedly and placed both my hands on his shoulders, allowing them to roam freely across his soft skin.

The bleeding hadn't entirely stopped yet on my palm and left trails of blood on him, but he didn't seem to care. He continued to kiss his way down my body.

He hooked two fingers in my G-string and nearly tore it off. I watched him move lower and place a kiss on my hood, spreading the lips of my pussy, sliding his tongue right down the center.

I jolted in response, releasing a soft moan. His bloodied palm flattened against my clit as he began licking me softly, barely making contact. I squirmed in frustration causing him to laugh. I reached down and slid my hands into his hair, letting the soft strands glide through my fingers as I pulled his face deeper between my legs.

He put his tongue all the way inside me and worked it up and down.

I moaned loudly, letting my head fall back on the bed.

His palm began to rotate, working my clit in a circular motion as he alternated between eating my pussy and teasing the swollen nub with the tip of his tongue.

I knew his blood was mixing with my arousal and the visual pushed me closer to the edge. Ciaran slipped a hand up my body and flattened it against my navel to keep me still. His mouth closed over my clit, and he softly began to suck. I came within seconds, crying out and cursing at the ceiling.

When he began to move back up, I cupped his face in my hands for the first time and marveled at how perfect it was as I guided his mouth back to mine. The taste of me and him combined had another moan trapped between our lips.

He indulged me, deepening the kiss as he reached for the drawer of the nightstand.

My stomach flipped again when I heard the crinkle of a wrapper.

He rolled the condom on and then took hold of my legs, placing them over his shoulders. He stared down at me and pressed forward, easing the head of his cock inside me.

I sucked in a breath and before I could release it, he thrust and buried himself fully, breaking the small barrier of innocence I never cared for. I cried out from surprise and shock, pleasure and pain mixing together as my body worked to accommodate the size of him. There was an overwhelming fullness and pleasurable burn as he stretched me.

"You, okay?" he questioned, his husky voice strained.

"Keep going," I implored, wrapping my hands around his biceps.

He pulled out and thrust back in, repeating the motion twice before he started to fuck me in earnest.

His thrusts were hard and measured, stroking deep inside my pussy. The sound of skin slapping against skin and my uninhibited moans began to echo around the room. His headboard rocked into the wall, creating a rapid rhythmic soundtrack.

"Damn, you feel good," he ground out, fucking me harder. His fingers knotted in my hair, gripping it tightly near the scalp. My pussy clenched from the bite of pain. I blinked to clear the water from my eyes.

He came down on top of me, letting my legs slide from his shoulders to his forearms, his thick cock going impossibly deeper as he fucked me harder. I clawed at his back and cried out his name. He nipped my ear and licked around its shell. "Keep screaming my name, Puppet. Scream it until you never forget who you belong to."

His hand wrapped around my throat and began to steadily apply pressure as he continued thrusting.

Another climax began to build, coming much faster than the first had. When it hit, my vision blurred as sparks of pleasure rushed through my veins. I came so loud I knew everyone in the entire apartment heard us.

I was still coming when Ciaran cursed under his breath and buried himself to the hilt, finding his own release. He kissed my forehead before resting his head on top of mine. I realized only one of us was breathing as if they'd run a marathon and it wasn't the person who'd done all the work.

I laid beneath him trying to get my thoughts in order, unsure of what I was supposed to do next. Ciaran didn't strike me as the cuddling type and that certainly wasn't lovemaking. It was plain and simple fucking. It was amazing—he knew exactly what to do to me and how.

It almost seemed like he'd studied me enough that he had it down to a science.

That or we were in sync. While both of those thoughts were somewhat disconcerting they didn't upset me.

I slightly lifted my head and placed a quick peck on his lips. He closed his eyes and released a soft sigh. Still unsure what to do now I reached up and began to pat his back. I didn't know if his sigh meant he was angry at himself, regretful, or deep in thought.

His shoulders started to shake, and I froze for a second before I realized he was laughing.

"What the fuck are you doing?"

"I...I don't know. Offering comfort?" I replied questioningly, beginning to laugh at my idiocy.

He pulled out and rolled onto his back, dragging me into his arms.

When I opened my eyes, I blinked a few times so that they adjusted to the lack of light. I sat up slowly, holding one hand to my brow and the other to the blanket.

My body ached similar to the way it had after that fateful evening of June sixteenth, but for a much more pleasurable reason. I reached for my phone and then remembered Maverick had taken it. I didn't know what time it was. Ciaran had finally let me tap out after round three, but it didn't feel like I'd slept more than twenty minutes.

I looked over at the beautifully enigmatic man beside me. The blanket covered his lower half, but now that my eyes had adjusted, I could see the cuts and definition of his upper body.

In clothes he was gorgeous, out of them he was like a completely different specimen. I couldn't compare him to anyone else. Not even a celebrity came to mind.

I rolled my lips together to smother a groan and pulled my knees up, resting my arms on them as I stared across the room, shivering from the chill in the air.

I couldn't believe I was here in this bed with an oath marking my flesh. No one would understand how significant this was unless they lived the lives we did. The reasoning for it, however, was deeply upsetting. Ciaran had said it best earlier.

I came from a world of dark secrets, yet I had never realized so many were being kept from me.

Until now.

I felt like my entire life was a fucking joke. My heart hurt when I thought of my siblings and *Abuelo*. Were we not close enough for them to warn me?

There was a heaviness in my chest that made me want to dig inside myself and remove the things that made me feel too much.

My parents...I hated them, but a part of me still loved them too. I hated that more.

I didn't know if they were selfish and cruel or if I was too weak for allowing anyone into the small space that I reserved for those I loved.

My eyes burned with unshed tears I quickly extinguished with the heel of my hands. I wouldn't sit around crying or torturing myself with self-pity. That would be beneficial for no one.

A feather-light touch pulled me from my thoughts as Ciaran ran his fingers down my spine. I looked over at him thankful we were in the dark. He wouldn't have seen my disconcertion.

"It's always hard to accept," he mused quietly. His hand fell away as he moved into a sitting position, bracing his back against the remaining pillows that lined the headboard. We'd knocked the rest onto his bedroom floor.

"What's hard?" I asked softly.

"Everything that comes with being an heir to families like ours. We're born to slaughter and accumulate power."

I slightly puckered my lips, turning that over in my head. I'd only known about the latter part. Power begot power, or whatever my father liked to say. He left out a few important pieces of information during that speech.

Ciaran remained quiet for a minute as if considering his next words. "The game is designed to strip away your humanity. For those watching it's a source of entertainment. The same concept doesn't apply to those who are forced into it.

"You weren't supposed to be in that category. Neither was my brother for entirely different reasons. He should have never gotten involved in this part of our world at all."

I slid back on the bed and positioned myself beside him, tucking the blanket beneath my arms. "Was it hard for you to accept?"

"I was raised to embrace the darkest parts of myself *and* our society," he laughed lightly and added, "I enjoy it too much."

I grinned with a breathy laugh. "Hm, why am I not surprised?"

"It can get tedious. I've been doing it for so long that there's hardly any excitement anymore."

"So, you're into murder and politics. Our missing siblings aside, this conversation probably should have happened before I wound up in your bed."

"You were going to end up in my bed because I wanted you here and I do whatever is necessary to get what I want."

I blew out a scoff.

"You don't think so?" he questioned with genial curiosity.

"Ciaran, honestly? No. I think it would have been unacted upon desire we'd be forced to bury when our parents told us who we had to marry."

His brisk laugh had a scowl furrowing my brow.

"My parents didn't dictate who I would be with. I expected them too, was prepared for it. And then I met you. Yours like to think they can control that decision still, but I never would've let that happen."

Denial came quick and steadfast. He was making it sound as if me being his was never a question, but a guarantee. I recalled his words at the party, that it was inevitable.

I hadn't jumped ahead of myself and started planning a future with him. He reached over and took the hand with the lines of our oath into his. "It worked out that you wanted me too. Otherwise, I would've had to make you eventually feel the same after I took what was mine."

My brows rose and my head swiveled in his direction. His sinister omissions were always worded as factual. He wouldn't settle for less even if what he wanted wasn't meant to be his. I didn't entirely dislike this side of him. It gave me an odd sense of belonging.

He brought my palm to his mouth and kissed it gently. "You feel a little better now?"

"Do I...? What do you mean?"

"You're hurting."

Understanding donned and I instinctively looked away. It wasn't possible he'd seen my face when he woke up.

The room was too dark. I hadn't even been facing his direction. It threw me off-kilter having him in tune with my emotions. He knew me in a way that would allude we'd been close for far longer than this.

"Don't do that," he admonished and pulled me across the bed until my side was pressed against his.

"Don't hide ever hide from me. I would never judge you."

The ire and sincerity in his tone threatened the barrier I'd erected to keep myself protected. I wasn't used to this kind of unwavering devotion from anyone other than my sisters. A few weeks ago, my *abuelo*. I wasn't sure why he seemed to care so much.

For me, this all came about because of our shared interest in saving our siblings and dismantling the helm of the Serpines. Ciaran was making it abundantly clear he'd had me on his agenda before this situation arose.

I wouldn't deny I enjoyed what we'd done. I would never regret him being my first or doing the oath given the reasons behind it. Being next to him wasn't all bad either. It gave me a sense of comfortability I'd never had in this capacity.

When he talked to me during our intermissions I listened to every word.

We really were a lot alike.

All of this was a major problem.

I liked him more than I should've. I had no idea what the future held, but one thing was for certain. Ciaran and I were a tragedy waiting to happen. It would all be because of me. I was the tragic one. He had no flaws. He was perfectly twisted.

I was still trying to find my way down the path I thought I'd begun to pave. This major deviation shined a light down on it and showed I hadn't really gotten anywhere. I wasn't going to give up, but he was lightyears ahead of me.

"You're doing it again."

"Will *you* not do that again?" I tried to pull away from him and his grip immediately tightened around my hand.

"Stop letting you be alone? No. I suggest you get the fuck over it. You're stuck with me until death and every lifetime after."

My jaw slackened. I slowly shook my head back and forth. "Ciaran, we can't have a secret...thing for the rest of our lives. You said you'd help me and somehow, I'm an asset to you. That's it."

"That's it?" he repeated back with an edge in his tone. "I'm not sure what kind of bullshit is going on inside that beautiful head, but this isn't a *thing.* Do you honestly think I needed an oath of this magnitude to help you?"

"No, but you'd need leverage for me to agree to it," I argued.

"If I wanted leverage, I can think of a million different ways to get it."

All of this was ringing true. He hadn't needed the oath to help me, but I'd misunderstood something in the translation and believed it was, in fact, for leverage until one second ago.

"Are you hellbent on repeating history that's still playing out in a very bad way?"

"What I am is fucking obsessed with you."

"You're *obsessed* with me?"

"To the point that I used to think of nothing but fucking or killing you, but then I started to like you, so I decided it was better to keep you alive and by my side."

I leaned away and stared at him. He'd admitted that so casually like it was an everyday topic of conversation.

"Eventually we'll fall in love," he added after making note of my expression.

I almost laughed. I wasn't sure he could fall in love. Ciaran had some stellar psychopathic tendencies. He couldn't be a full-blown psycho because he did seem capable of loving.

He could feel something close to remorse as well if his attitude towards his brother was anything to go off.

I wasn't the most stable person up top and had a moral compass that occasionally stopped ticking, so I couldn't judge. As for this plan he had concocted? I didn't know where to begin with that.

"Have you perhaps forgotten I'm a Serpine? Those snakes you hate so much?"

"You're not a snake, you never have been." He pulled me closer until his face was a breath away from mine. "The only thing that you are now is mine."

Trying to temper the pounding of my heart, I let my eyes dip to his lips, flying back up when I realized those were too much of a distraction. "I don't understand."

"I know. Right now, you don't need to" He settled back against the headboard and guided my head to his chest.

I didn't know how to navigate the minefield of this situation. There were so many complexities to sort through.

"Are we sure we can do this?"

"We are doing this," he assured me, his husky voice seeping into my consciousness. I briefly closed my eyes, and he ran a hand through my hair. "I've got you, Puppet. I promise."

I let myself feel the safety of his embrace and then lifted my head and peered up at him. "What happens now?"

"Now?" He reached down and gripped my ass, maneuvering me until I was straddling him. "Now I teach you how to play at the Devil's Playground."

CHAPTER NINE

My life did not get any easier after making a deal with the devil. If anything, the months thereafter were ten times harder. I felt like I'd gotten the lead in a Broadway-worthy play and if I made a single error then that would be it—curtains closed. The problem was no one gave me a script. I was doing the best with what I had, and I didn't have much.

Resting an elbow on the dining room table, I studied the calendar on my phone. I was trying to pinpoint Lamia's due date and couldn't narrow down exactly how far along she was. I'd had no news of her since the night of the oath. Ciaran had recently become radio silent too, for longer than he usually did.

The last time we saw one another was an event I'd been forced to attend for some fundraising event, raising money for a restaurant called *Blight House* or something. I'd pretended nothing had changed between us and that was a feat in itself.

I'd heard long-distance relationships were hard. I would take one of those over the one I had to hide from the world. There were no texts, emails, or letters to re-read during times of longing. You didn't have a phone call to look forward to. Even whispered conversations could be overheard.

Our time together came with thorough detailed planning of overnight excursions I never actually went to. Instead, I was off with him and our friends. What was dating when you were having an illicit affair that ensured you'd be decoding riddles and learning the many ways to survive hell on earth?

The downside was how we had to space everything out to keep from being caught. It had become one of the hardest parts of all this. I expected hardships. I never thought one of them would be missing him

Aside from the faded lines on my palm the only memento and proof of our relationship was the copy of the photo he'd brought me a few weeks ago, the one from the night of Sainte's party. I stashed it in a secret space inside my bathroom for safekeeping.

I understood now why Lamia had risked everything for a relationship that would never be accepted by anyone aligned with the Serpines. I was doing the same damn thing. I wondered if that made us selfish.

I wouldn't change a thing, regardless. Over the past few months despite how hard it was being in such a complex relationship Ciaran had taught me a lot.

Dormant demons I'd always carried were starting to wake.

I'd never felt better about myself. He made me see things in a new light. I knew I was capable of rising up and taking everything away from those who'd hurt me and making it my own.

I wouldn't be alone, but it was nice to realize I wasn't as powerless as I'd believed. Nights together always ended with our bodies tangled together. It didn't matter how grueling his 'lessons' were. We needed the physical connection.

Hearing the click of Pandora's heels, I exited the calendar app I'd begun staring at while lost in thought and did a quick check of my texts, frowning when I saw there'd still been no reply from Mel or Grace.

Pandora breezed into the dining room with a smile on her face. "Sorry, *hija*. I got caught up on a phone call with *Papá*."

"It's fine." I eyed her suit outfit. "Is he okay? He's been gone for a while."

She sat her cellphone on the table and waved off my concern, reaching for the cloth napkin that went over her lap. "He's good. A lot of higher-ups had to fly out and see our new build site."

"Mm." I nodded as if I truly cared about this city they were reconstructing. They never told me enough information about their work for me to become invested.

The longer Matheus stayed gone the better. Living in this house with my family was a daily battle of wills. I reached for more Caesar dressing and drizzled some across already saturated lettuce.

I'd been working on this salad for fifteen minutes. I had little desire to do these luncheons and even less of an appetite as I pretended that we were normal.

"Did you know Ciaran Belair had a brother?" she asked without seeming particularly interested in the topic. It was an act I knew well.

If I hadn't been so on guard, I would've choked on the baby tomato I'd just bitten into. I chewed as I normally would and then wiped my mouth. "No. Haven't his parents been married forever? Did someone cheat?"

Pandora began tapping away at the screen of her cellphone, sliding it across the table towards me. "Watch this."

"What is it?"

"Watch," she urged with an airy laugh. "I want to know your thoughts."

Unsure what I was about to see, I took a mental breath and hit play on the video. The speaker immediately erupted with intelligible shouting. It wasn't a perfectly clear video. Certain aspects were blurred but it looked to have been done purposely, not a quality issue. I could make out at least three people in masks. There must have been a fourth because as they chased a group of people through the woods the camera bounced.

One person specifically drew my attention. My mouth went dry, a heaviness spreading through my chest as her features became more evident. The video momentarily cleared as someone off-camera fired an arrow. A guy with a striking resemblance to Ciaran grabbed my sister and pulled her out of its path.

The arrow found a mark in one of the girls that had been running with them, slamming into her temple with such impact it came out on the other side. Whoever was recording had gotten close enough by this point that I saw the blood and something resembling a sponge be expelled from the hole the tip of the arrow had formed.

The tomato I'd just eaten was suddenly much too acidic. I blindly reached for my water, watching as the girl staggered. When the camera panned to a side profile view, I recognized her too.

I swallowed a gasp as Lamia's best friend disappeared into a patch of thick overgrowth. The video cut off abruptly, silencing my sister's hysterical screaming.

I went through no less than four emotions in the span of a few seconds, ending with rage. I swallowed repeatedly and took another pull from my glass.

"Did you know Ciaran had a brother?" she repeated her prior question with no vocal inflection to hint at her mood as she reached across the table and took back her phone.

That's what she wanted to lead with? Not an explanation why her pregnant daughter was being hunted down by masked psychopaths?

My pulse was racing so face I felt it throbbing in my neck. I couldn't articulate words. When I could finally speak, I was unable to keep the fury from my voice. "Where is she?"

"She was on an island. It's been shut down for the time being. There are talks to bring it back in a few years. It depends on how well this next project does."

I sat back in my chair and stared at the woman across from me. She was speaking of her in the past tense, and as casually as us discussing her day at the office. If I had any doubts about my family knowing why Lamia went off the grid, Pandora just cleared them all up.

"How could you do this to her?"

"She did this to herself, my love. Haven't I always told you every choice you make big or small will matter at some point or another? We gave her a choice and she chose the island. Between you and I, be glad she isn't of the time our next venture will be. She'd never have made it."

"She's *your* daughter."

Her brown eyes lost a bit of their light at the reminder. "You're my daughter too."

Clearing her throat, she sprinkled parmesan cheese on her plate of food and picked up a fork. "I'm surprised Ciaran didn't tell you all of this. That video isn't recent."

I wasn't going to engage in her wordplay about him. She could be lying or twisting the truth to pit me against him. I tried to think of what I should do, and how to handle this. Dealing with Pandora, I knew she'd be steps ahead of me and already implementing a countermeasure.

My parents didn't get where they were by sitting on their hands or going on the defense. I couldn't text or call anyone for help. I was on my own right now.

"Why did you show me that video?"

"In light of recent events we've decided it was time for you to know the fate of the girl so we can move on."

The *we've* was a unified front with the rest of my family. She would never act without first conferring with them.

My fingers wanted to curl into the arm of my chair. I kept them relaxed and held my composure. Pandora tilted her head to the side and offered a slight smile. "You've gotten better."

"What the fuck is wrong with you?"

Her brows lifted in response to my language. She didn't care if I swore like a sailor, but it was never allowed to be directed at her. That would be too disrespectful.

"I'll let that go because I know you're angry. I've been in the same exact situation. It does get easier. I lost two daughters, Liliana. I'm not particularly joyous about this. I refuse to lose a third. You might hate me now, but I promise I'm doing this because I *love* you."

Shockingly, she did seem genuinely upset about this. But I didn't understand anything else she was talking about. Wasn't *I* the second daughter?

"If you don't like it then why are you doing it?"

"Because even someone as affluent as I must acquiesce to the syndicate's rules," she replied with a touch of bitterness.

What kind of monarchy bullshit was this? She gave me a tight smile and reached for her own glass of water. "I should have been more careful. I thought you'd be fine enjoying life like a normal girl."

"Normal?" I echoed disbelievingly. "Nothing about my life has ever been normal."

"You couldn't be kept completely ignorant of certain aspects, no. Your initiation would be a disaster and over before it began if we sheltered you completely."

What initiation? I began to crack, running my hands over my face in frustration, pulling in a deep breath of air.

If I countered with every question that I had, we'd be here for the next two years. "I don't know half of what you're saying. So why don't you tell me what you want Pandora."

Her features became pinched with a deep frown. I'd never called her by name before and it clearly struck a nerve. "You really let that vile boy get to you."

"At least he told me the truth."

She laughed derisively.

"Oh, *Hija*. I'd never aim to trample your heart, but a rule of thumb is that men are never as transparent as they pretend to be." Shaking her head, she reached into the pocket of her suit. "I thought you knew better. I blame myself too, I see now where I went wrong which is we're both going to do better."

She removed a bottle of pills and sat them on the table between us.

There was no name or label for me to discern what they were. I looked from them to her questioningly.

"We're going to start over. It won't be pleasant at first but in the long run, you won't remember that."

"What do you mean? What are those for?"

"That's nothing but a means to an end. The real work starts with ECT and sessions with a crew of highly qualified individuals that only work for our family."

I sat taller, preparing to bolt from the table if necessary.

Every word out of her mouth painted a grim picture of my indefinite future.

"You want to experiment on me?"

"Absolutely not!" she objected as if genuinely offended. "This is a tried and so far, true method that we've been using for close to a year if the individual is worth it. A few of your friends from Sainte's have already begun the process. Melantha and Gracelyn will be joining as well. Your compliance would do them wonders."

In the end, it was the mention of them that stopped me from doing anything rash. Her threat was wrapped in faux words of encouragement. They hadn't been texting back because their families had already moved on them.

"How did you know about Sainte's?" I found myself asking.

"A birdie came and told me all about it a few weeks ago. I'm proud of you, by the way."

Her praise meant fuck all to me. I wanted to know who came running to her and why. Weeks? It had been months since that night. I swallowed a bite of lettuce that tasted like lead. There were only six people that survived Judicium. That left three possible choices.

Gnawing my inner cheek, the severity of this situation began to sink in. In an attempt to help my sister, I'd screwed myself. Or maybe this wasn't about Lamia at all.

"Is this family feud really worth all of this?"

"They've taken enough from me." She looked into my eyes to drive home her answer. "You have no idea what was done. It's like history keeps repeating itself and every time the ending is a goddamn tragedy."

Upon hearing those words, a sense of Deja-Vu swept over me. I'd had a thought of this same degree months ago. I was a tragedy waiting to happen. That was coming to fruition at the expense of the people I loved.

I looked around the room, turning that over in my head. "What exactly are you going to do to me?"

"Your family won't be doing anything but guiding you through reprogramming. We want you partially ready for what's to come. Your medical team is responsible for removing the bad memories."

I laughed incredulously. "You're going to remove my memories?"

"Most people always have that reaction. I'd say you'll see, but you won't even remember this conversation happened."

She was being serious.

I wanted to say she was full of shit, but I knew that wasn't likely the case.

With the right people and method, I'm sure it could be done. Worse, Mel and Grace had already been dragged into this.

"Why do we have to forget?" I asked quietly.

"His true intentions will break you in the end if he doesn't kill you himself. You're not going to let that happen."

"What do *you* know about his intentions?"

She didn't elaborate, simply took a few more bites of her food. I was beginning to understand something had happened at some point between her and the Belairs. That didn't give her the right to project her trauma onto me.

It didn't erase the fact she dumped my sister somewhere to be killed. She spoke about her in the past tense, I refused to believe she was dead. It wasn't a possibility I was willing to accept.

As for Ciaran, I knew he wasn't being wholly honest with me from the beginning, but he would never kill me. He made me feel safe whenever I was by his side. This entire time he was making sure I would survive.

My conflict came with the knowledge she wanted the same thing. Everyone was lying and hiding something. They wanted me for different reasons, and I only wanted freedom. No, that wasn't entirely true. I couldn't say I didn't want him too.

As if sensing the direction of my thoughts, Pandora studied me with something that looked like sadness in her eyes. "At least you won't remember the heartbreak." With a quick exhalation, she composed herself and motioned to the pill bottle. "You can take one after you finish eating or I can call in the men waiting outside to give you the first dose. I hope we can do this the easy way. I don't want you in pain even if it will be forgotten."

She was so adamant someone was going to get inside my head and remove the things they had no rights to. I'd be lying if I said I wasn't somewhat terrified. My mind had always been my own. It's what made me who I was.

Arguing this seemed to be a moot point, she'd already come to a decision and was waiting for me to make mine. Robotically, I reached for my fork again, giving her my answer without words. I knew this wasn't a battle I could win, but that didn't mean I'd lose the war. No matter what happened to me I held firm to the belief that I would never fully lose myself.

Melantha and Gracelyn, there was no way they'd break them either. Mel was one of the strongest people I knew, and Grace never got enough credit. I only hoped this didn't destroy the part of her I wanted to protect.

They'd been dragged into this mess because of me. I don't think that was a guilt that could ever be erased. Some things stuck with you, always.

That brought small comforts from what my family didn't seem to know. They didn't have any idea of who I really was. It would be a grave lapse of judgement if they truly believed I'd become what they wanted me to be. I would never accept a delusive destiny.

Matters of the soul were even riskier. You couldn't take that away from someone or change their genetic makeup. It seemed I was born with tragedy in my blood. That could be as much of a blessing as it was a curse. When it came time for me to bleed, I would turn their whole world upside down and use it as a throne.

There was one person I could count on to help me when all was said and done. Someone I knew I'd never truly forget.

Ciaran Belair

He had my heart in the palm of his murderous hands. By everything tainted and maleficent, we're forever bonded.

He promised he'd never let me go.

I believed him.

CHAPTER TEN

I watched her from a distance.

She glanced at me once when she did a sweep of her surroundings, but it was nothing but a passing glance as she pushed a cart down the travel aisle, walking in my direction. There was a tattoo on her arm that she hadn't had before.

Someone had covered the scar she'd gotten from Judicium. It had been faint, but I suppose her parents didn't want her to notice it was there. That would require a backstory of where it came from.

I let myself drink in the sight of her as I had been from the time she resurfaced. She was healthy and fit.

I could probably bounce change off her ass. Her physical attributes hadn't been altered in any way besides those few things.

She was as breathtaking to me as she'd always been. I resisted the urge to drag her ass out of this store and lock her away. There was too much at stake for that. While she'd been hidden away from our world, it still kept turning.

Someone else needed me now and I wasn't going to let her down like I had Puppet. I wouldn't let her down again either. There was a list of people that would be joining her on this trip and none of them would be returning. It was the tip of the metaphorical iceberg of amends.

I looked over my shoulder to make sure Kyrous hadn't gotten his ass out of the car and followed us into the store. We hadn't been back in the real world all too long and he needed time to assimilate.

The last thing I needed was him strolling through the store in search of his next victim.

He damn sure didn't need to see the blonde a few feet away, laughing at something someone out of sight was saying.

Lana paused in front of a pack of sanitizing wipes and began to compare them with the others. Was this what fucking shopping consisted of? I couldn't tell you the last time I'd gone into a store like this. That's what hired help was for. What was she comparing?

I knew for a fact her family kept her bank account stacked these days, so money wasn't an issue. I'd been pissed when I first saw the numbers. It meant she'd pleased them enough for an allowance.

"I think I'm nervous," Maverick mumbled.

"Don't be such a pussy, you don't even have to speak," Charon retorted.

Melantha came around the corner and called Liliana's name.

She turned away from the wipes and caught something Melantha had just tossed to her.

"Mel," she hissed, holding the box to her chest as Grace laughed at them.

As I got closer I was able to get a glimpse of the packaging. Were those condoms?

"You never know what could happen," Melantha reasoned.

"The fuck?"

At the sound of my voice, my puppet turned and looked at me. I watched as surprise and confusion flashed across her beautiful face before a guarded expression wiped both away.

I didn't like that.

She was mine. I was hers. It was that simple. She wasn't allowed to be fucking guarded with me.

If I were to bend her over that shopping cart and fuck her right here, would she remember the way my dick felt when it was inside her?

I wanted to reach out and touch her hair. It looked softer than I remembered. I wanted to wrap her in my arms and see if she felt as safe as she used to in my embrace. That was the very reason I didn't. She didn't know who I was yet.

Why the fuck did I let this happen? Their families made sure we were away on business before making the move to lock the girls up. Their location had been top-secret until it was too late to do anything. By the time we found where they were being kept, they'd already had their brains rewired.

It was fucked what had been to them. I knew grown men that wouldn't have been able to endure. They would've cracked much sooner than they had.

I wouldn't be letting it go even after I had her back. I had names and none of them were safe.

Liliana shoved the box of condoms onto a nearby shelf and breezed by us with her cart, polite enough to excuse herself.

Fuck if that didn't burn.

Melantha followed without sparing us anything but a cursory glance. There may have been a flicker of recognition in her eyes, but she didn't react to it. Gracelyn at least smiled, but she always fucking smiled. Ky was going to devour this girl and then spit out whatever was left when he was done.

At the end of the aisle, Puppet looked back at me with another flash of confusion. That was all I'd needed to see. I hadn't come here to speak to her or demand she remembered me. I wasn't that fucking obtuse.

This wasn't the time for that either. I hadn't approached her to ease my consciousness, that was already damned. I came to obtain something and succeeded.

"Are you good?" Charon asked, preparing to offer moral support.

"Yeah, I got what I needed."

We left the store and began prepping for an appointment we'd taken the liberty of scheduling ourselves.

You expected top-notch security in a building like this. We bypassed the locking mechanism on the entrance and strolled right in without anyone there to stop us.

Even at this hour, our building would be impossible to enter with such ease and it stood fifteen stories high directly across the street.

My mom had agreed on the location so that she could piss off the Serpines bright and early every morning.

The black glass windows reflected the glow of Maverick's mask as he made a show of looking around the spacious lobby. "Is this stupidity or arrogance?"

"Probably a bit of both."

"He knew we were going to come, right?" Charon asked, shifting the black case in his hands.

"Only one way to find out."

We walked towards the north wing, slowing when a loan guard entered from the east. He froze at the sight of us, his eyes going round with fear.

"Hey, how you doing tonight?" Charon playfully queried.

"You need to leave." The man went for his radio and then must have thought better of it, going for the gun on his hip instead.

"I'll meet you upstairs," Kyrous remarked, making his way towards the guard.

"Stay back!" the man drew his gun and leveled it at Ky's chest.

That wasn't enough to stop him.

"You're not going to shoot me," Ky monotoned. He walked right up to the guy and grabbed his arm, bending it at an unnatural angle to point the gun away from him. At the same time, he grabbed the man by the throat, cutting his scream down to a garble.

Leaving him to handle the guard, I continued through the lobby. "Leave him alive, Ky," I tossed over my shoulder.

We approached the elevators, and I used the key card our tech guy had made to grant us usage. Once we were inside, I let it flit between my fingers to land on the slate floor so Kyrous could use it when he was done with the guard.

"The top?" Maverick asked.

"Straight to the top," I confirmed.

The doors slid shut and he hit the button. We didn't encounter anyone else on our way to the top.

We passed floor thirteen where the Astaroth offices were, Gracelyn's family. The Lamashtu where Melantha's worked on floor fourteen, and then finally our ride stopped, and the doors slid apart. Another lobby of sorts awaited us.

Frosted glass doors with two silver handles in the shape of an S complete with red jewels were a small boast of the Serpines wealth and power. If I didn't come from a family just as powerful with powerful friends, I might have been impressed.

Most of the lights were off. Only a few wall sconces had been left on, giving the space an intimate glow. We crossed the partial lobby and through the doors.

I didn't waste time sight-seeing and went straight to where we needed to be.

When we walked into the office of Amon Serpine, he didn't look the least bit surprised to see us. As suspected, he knew we'd be coming just not when. I was a little disappointed I hadn't been able to surprise the old man.

"You boys don't know how to knock?"

"Isn't the surprise better if we don't?" Maverick countered.

He grunted and sat back in his large leather chair. His brown eyes took in our outfits, lingering for a second on the masks. "You might as well sit down. Drink? Or are the masks staying on?"

"We're good," I answered for both questions.

"Eh, suit yourself." He reached for the bottle of whiskey sitting near the edge of his desk and poured a decent amount into a glass he'd already been drinking from.

We settled onto the U-shaped sectional across from his desk and Charon placed the case he was holding on his lap.

Amon looked at it with a slight twist of his mouth. His grandchildren were the perfect mix of him. I could see pieces of both Liliana and her brother in his face.

"If you knew we were coming, you know why I'm here."

"Is no if kid. I had the building all but freely accessible for weeks now waiting on you to get your asses up to my office."

"You never heard of a phone, old man?" Charon questioned, throwing in a jab of his own.

"You're going to help me secure your granddaughter's hand."

His brows slightly rose. "You must mean in the eyes of the syndicate because we all know you've marked my Lilly in every other way."

He had to of been referring to the oath. I wasn't sure how he knew of it when not even Liliana's parents were aware. Their rat hadn't been informed about that. To make sure he wasn't having any doubts of its validity, I motioned to Charon.

He popped open the black case he was carrying and lifted the lid before turning it around so that Amon could see what was inside.

"We've got the game covered for the first two phases. After the gig is up, we may need your help. This is on top of you ensuring me and your granddaughter are engaged."

Kyrous came strolling into the room just as I finished speaking and sat down beside Charon. There was a dot of blood on his mask. I could guarantee he didn't listen and killed the guard downstairs. He was moody as fuck these days.

"What made you so sure I'd help you?"

I laughed derisively. "If you don't help us what good are you to me? Because if you don't help us, you're turning your back on Liliana."

"That's not--."

"If you don't help us, you'll be a thing of the past when I hand her the match to burn this whole fucking empire to the ground so she can rebuild her own."

"You see where he's going with this?" Maverick chimed in. "If you don't help, you're fucked."

Amon examined the vials of blood inside the case with a bleak expression. I wasn't sure if it was from him struggling with my ultimatum or something else. I didn't feel any sympathy for him, but I wouldn't want to be in this same position. He'd have to betray his family and each one of their alliances.

It was for a more than worthy cause.

We all knew that this was the best decision for everyone partaking in this secret meeting and more importantly, his granddaughters. With or without his compliance things were set in motion for the biggest event of the year.

I didn't give a fuck about the history between my father and Pandora. Neither did he. He had let it go until the crazy bitch got my brother involved in her personal vendetta. That made it harder for Puppet's grandfather to turn down my deal.

Three of the most prominent families the syndicate had were backing it. He sighed deeply and took one final look at the vials from the night of the oath. We'd bottled it for insurance purposes back then and kept them stashed away.

It was one of the smartest things I had ever done. All he needed to do was test the blood to make sure it matched Puppet's if any doubts surfaced.

"Why are only two of the girls included?"

"We knew they were a package deal, but two is still better one, don't you think?"

"And my brother would have thrown a fit otherwise. Nobody wants that," Charon added, clapping Ky on the shoulder.

"Why my Liliana?"

She wasn't fucking his. I bit back that retort and grinned. "Puppet knows who pull her strings."

His bushy brows slammed together in confusion that had my grin widening even though he couldn't see it. I didn't need him to understand my meaning.

The ones that mattered did.

She did too. That look of confusion told me something inside her still knew who I was. Her family wanted to take what I already deemed belonged to me. She was mine. To fuck. To protect. And use to bring the Serpines to an end.

She was everything to me.

Her grandfather nodded once, and elation spread through my chest. "They leave for their trip in two weeks. I'll have their necklaces to them before then. Is that enough time for you to do what you need?"

"I'm already ten steps ahead." I leaned forward and braced my hands on his desk. "You wouldn't happen to have a knife preference, would you? We've already got one prepped."

EPILOGUE

The nights we had together should've been impossible to forget.

It's not her fault she doesn't remember.

It was *them* who made sure she forgot.

They eradicated me from her mind, not doing shit to ensure she was gone from mine, too.

And that's where they fucked up.

As if that wasn't a death-worthy violation in itself, they went a step further and destroyed one of their own. The Serpines and everyone in their inner circle deserved everything that was coming to them.

But where was the fun in letting them off easy?

For years, we'd been watching.

Learning and plotting.

We remained obedient and kept our distance. All of that was now a thing of the past. I had the only permission I needed to keep Liliana by my side.

The two of us together was a nightmare in the making. What could be more beautiful than a bond formed from blood and chaos, blessed by the ones that worshipped everything below?

I was ready to take this game to a higher level. The clock was ticking, and when it hit zero nothing was going to be the same.

It was time for my puppet to wake up and remember who she was.

They wanted a show that would go down in history, I was going to make sure they got one.

DAEMONIUM

Pre-order here.

https://mybook.to/daemonium

Ky & Gracelyn's book

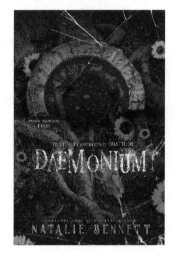

CARMINE

Dark MFM Standalone

More books from Natalie Bennett

The Badlands series: Complete

Savages

Deviants

Outcasts

Heathens

Badlands Next Generation: Ongoing

Degenerates

Hellions

Renegades

Miscreants

Misfits: 2023

The Dahlia Saga

Malice

Obscene

Depravity

Malevolence

Iniquity

Debauchery: 2023

Coveting Delirium Duet: Complete

Opaque Melodies

Melodic Madness

<u>Old Money Trilogy: Complete</u>

Queen of Diamonds

King of Hearts

Ace of Spades

<u>Pretty Lies, Ugly Truths Duet: Complete</u>

Sweet Poisons

Sick Remedies

<u>Stygian Isle: Standalones</u>

Del Diablo

Muerte: 2023

<u>Bitter & Sick Duet</u>

Twelve of Roses: prequel

Thorns of Roses: late 2023

TOR: TBA

<u>Reign & Ruin Trilogy: Complete</u>

Lawless Kingdom

Savage Gods

Vicious Dynasty

<u>A Game of Villains: Coming Soon</u>

Carmine

<u>City of Gods</u>

Pestilence

Books from Mae Royal

Dark PNR & Fantasy

<u>Kings of Terror: Reverse Harem Duet</u>

Bride of Demonio

Queen of Demonio

<u>A Curse of Beauty & Ruin</u>

A Curse of Beauty & Ruin

THE SECT

An exclusive subscription for sneak peeks, book news, and freebies

Join <u>HERE</u>

NEFARIOUS

Get early reveals, exclusive giveaways, and talk all the bookish things!

Join my reader's group HERE

SOCIALS

Instagram

authornataliebennett

@authormroyal

Pinterest

@authornbennett

Facebook

/nataliebennettwriter

Website

www.nbennett.net

Tiktok

@natbennettauthor

Made in the USA
Columbia, SC
20 June 2024

37290511R00143